NUMBLAND ⊕ SECURITY
THE SERIES

NUMBLAND SECURITY ™

THE JOURNEY TO NOIHMLA

BOOK ONE

DAVID FURNEAUX

Published by Rover T Hill Productions LLC

Copyright © May 2018
By David Furneaux

All rights reserved. This is a work of fiction. All of the characters, organizations, and events in this novel are either products of the author's imagination or are used fictitiously.

No part of this book may be used or reproduced in any manner without written permission except in the case of brief quotations embodied in articles and reviews. Unauthorized reproduction of any part of this work is illegal and punishable by law.

Copyright © May 2018 David Furneaux
All rights reserved.

ISBN: 0-9991933-6-8
ISBN-13: 978-0-9991933-6-5

DEDICATION

To Teresa
For your love, dedication,
support, and believing in me.

CONTENTS

	Acknowledgments	i
1	Up the Mountain	1
2	Numbland Security	17
3	The River Crossing	25
4	Milo Pangloss	45
5	Outpost Jackson, Afghanistan	62
6	Tall, Beautiful and Dangerous	71
7	How Harry Won in '48	81
8	Summer 2000	90
9	The Reformation	101
10	Brad	109
11	The Foundation Brunch	118
12	The Catch	128
13	The President's Reception	140
14	Hatchet	148
15	Family Legacy	158
16	Out of the Woods	168
17	Loose Ends	180
18	Summer 2001	187
19	Back for the Last Year	206
20	9/11	219
21	Top Secret Clearance	237
22	Finality	258
	About the Author	
	Numbland Security Series	

ACKNOWLEDGMENTS

I want to express my sincere gratitude to so many people that helped on this journey.

To Mom and Dad. You showed us what love, perseverance, dedication, and service to country meant. To my wife, Teresa, whose love, dedication, patience, proofing, and belief in the project made it possible.

To Tom, who continues to work at making this a better country, long after you wore the uniform. To Ben, thank you for your love, support, wisdom, and advice. You make me proud every day.

To CBA and Pinto, thanks for urging me to do the book, the ideas, and the critiquing that made it better. You're both better satirists but probably still belong in the Fitless Protection Program. Jim and Deanna, thanks for being great friends, den mother, and charter Encore Film Society members. Lynn, Marlou, and Jan, thanks for reading and critiques.

To my Aunt Betty, thanks for being a coach, and loving mentor who told me to dream. To Harve, who made me believe I could tell veterans' stories. To Tom M. and Steve L., thanks for your life friendships. You both get the Army roots. To Dave T., thanks for being the coach and critic I needed. Fred, thank you for the romance novel advice.

To the IMMC life friends, thanks for being "friends that are there when it matters." To Penny and Lillian, thanks for being fans of satire. To our friends small group, thanks for your support and prayers during tough times. Mo, thanks for the advice and time. To Doug and Jan, thanks for the encouragement and advice. Donna, thanks for the insights. To Marty, thank you for the help and advice on early drafts. To Bob and Pam, thanks for making sure veterans' histories get saved.

To C.D., thanks for your service, for being there. From the space race through making sure we'd continue to function on 9/11. You're one of our great hidden heroes.

To Kammie, thanks for Inspired Grounds, a great meeting site for planning, editing, and coffee.

To Jen, thanks for telling me to go with Carrie as a smart, sarcastic, and beautiful volleyball star. To Susan, thanks for listening to the early concepts and to your folks, Keith and Kathie, thanks for your service in the military. To Katie, thanks for critiques and enthusiasm. To George and Kent, who could deliver a hilarious punch line better than any of us. To the NCOs, a salute to Tav, Florence, Brasel, and Foster. Thanks for your service, sacrifice, and sense of humor. And to George Poage and Tom Hamilton, thanks for being great work and life mentors.

Finally, a huge thank you to my editor and self-publishing expert, Beth Burgmeyer and Happy Jack Editing & Publishing. (happyjackpublishing.com). Without your help, advice, and sacrifice, this book and series could not have been published. You're a special person and a wonderful gift to writers.

1

Up the Mountain

FEBRUARY 2011

IN THE EARLY morning darkness, Carrie Station couldn't see the tree-covered mountain ahead off the highway. She often came early. It still had a haunting beauty before sun up. It didn't feel or look like she was in the D.C. area.

It's 1730 hours over there. Hope he's safe.

When she pulled off the exit then onto a country road, there it loomed. As she drove up the road among the trees, she thought how it had evolved since 9/11. The underground multi-agency site had been remodeled after it had been used on 9/11 as a safe bunker for key Congressional leaders. The site took up over 70 acres and over 80,000 square feet of space.

After clearing security and the retinal scan,

Carrie went down the elevator eight floors in the bunker complex. The unit and office were at the *Strategic Activities* level.

As she got back to her workstation, she said, "Morning J. Morning Harry." She gave her daily mock salute to an old black and white 8 x 10 photo of J. Edgar Hoover and Harry Truman—"The Boys"—near her desk.

When their unit's new manager, Steve, started two months ago, he asked, "Why do we have those two 'relics' in a picture by your workstation?"

"These are two of our models from past national security crises during World War II and the Cold War."

"Okay, good." he said.

"A week, later, he told me they were national security icons," laughed Kelly, his executive assistant and Carrie's best friend at work.

Carrie worked at the National Office of Intelligence, Homeland & Military Liaison Agency (NOIHMLA). It was an ultra-top-secret unit known only to the upper leadership of the key domestic, foreign intelligence units and their special congressional oversight committee. The oversight committee gave it the long, bland, 'federal-speak' title intentionally.

Carrie was fiercely dedicated to her work from both her beliefs and loss since 9/11. She did what she felt was best for NOIHMLA's narrow mission: *To keep the US safe from terrorist attacks through an effective yet more customer-friendly airline screening program.*

Carrie had grown with the government, contractors and industries that were part of adding over 250 new federal units, task forces, and agencies since 9/11. It had become a separate entity from the military industrial complex. She called it the National Intelligence/Terrorism Industry Complex (NI/TIC).

"Well guys, let's see what we have to deal with today," Carrie said to The Boys.

The Boys were Carrie's inside joke. Harry Truman was the Good Cop to J. Edgar Hoover's Bad Cop. When Harry didn't give J. Edgar the new CIA under his authority in '47, Hoover hated him and tried to undercut him from then on. J. Edgar used his access to FBI investigations and wiretapping (sometimes illegally) to coerce or blackmail political or public figures. If they opposed him, he'd call them soft on communism or crime much like some were now using soft on terrorism as a charge.

Harry Truman, as President, distrusted J. Edgar every day but had to live with him in a stalemate while trying to use the new powers of the growing post-WW II intelligence apparatus in the best, constitutional ways.

Carrie saw today's FBI as a great organization with occasional arrogance and mistakes, but a force for good, day in, day out.

For Carrie, The Boys were a yin and yang reminder to use her power with an incredible access to information carefully and appropriately.

Carrie's workstation had two rows of flat screen monitors. The first row of five screens was directly in front of her on her wide desk. They showed both stationary and rotating screens of airport passenger terminals around the US. Carrie watched passengers going through metal detectors and conveyor belt screening at four different airports with the security officers in view. The fifth screen showed the inside of a top-secret hangar in the D.C. area with a Gulfstream jet. This was her extra "pet."

The second row of screens was up on wall mounts. There were four large flat screens, high definition and in color. These four were for immediate awareness of breaking news on cable and network news stations. They could be switched to local or other sources during attacks and special events requiring a higher degree of security and alert levels. Carrie had requested these to connect the dots before, during, and after an attack.

As Senior Specialist, Level Five for NOIHMLA's *Air Travelers' and Security Officers' Fund for Training* (ATASOFT), it was her special job to watch the airline security screening system and help aid the process, where she and NOIHMLA felt appropriate.

"Okay, system shows we may have both a *GABA*

and a *DPC* at Chicago O'Hare today," Carrie said in a low whisper. "A daily double in Chicago."

GABA was a Gate Agent Behavior Adjustment prospect. DPC was a Disruptive Passenger Counseling prospect.

Carrie always tried to be fair to both the gate agents and passengers with problems "fitting in." When NOIHMLA was formed, she asked to go through new hire training with gate agents anonymously. Following that, she went on a six-week rotation through Atlanta, Chicago, LAX, Dallas/Ft. Worth, JFK in NY and Denver. It gave her a perspective on the daily challenges at that level.

"All quiet on the western front this morning?" Kelly asked as she walked past on the way to get coffee.

"No, a gate agent and passenger at O'Hare that may not fit," said Carrie. "Two more all-stars for The Fitless Protection Program."

◆◆◆

The two had travelled from their Saharan training camp to Central America, then in a tunnel under the southern US border, courtesy of the cartel. They paid with money to an offshore account along with a more valuable commodity the cartel had found they needed. A one-month contract with their terrorist cell's best social media expert and cyber specialist for hacking government and financial sites. The cartel had come to realize their brutal tactics and cash only bought so much when it came to the narco-terrorists' business of the future.

The travelers had brought a new plastic explosive from Yemen that had been through a dry run test on an African airline flight to Marseilles. It made it past the airline screeners and later was undetected by dogs at Marseilles luggage. Now they were going to be martyrs in the infidel's backyard.

◆ ◆ ◆

Carrie's laptop pinged. It was a "Ghost Passport" icon. Two passports of deceased US citizens from Texas had just been used at an auto-check kiosk at the San Antonio airport. Her unit had just received test software to integrate with facial ID software. It didn't set off alerts with the local airports yet because these two names were not on the "No Fly/Caution for Search" list at present.

"Kelly, can you drop off your Midwest screens, switch to San Antonio," Carrie said over their closed system headsets. "This is not a drill."

Carrie had dropped into her focused, calm, "Captain's voice." She was revered within the agencies for her ability to use emerging technology, new data bases, and human behavior hunches with an instinctive style that others marveled at…after the event.

"We've got two "Ghosts" flying from San Antonio to Dulles in D.C. I'm pulling up their pictures. The demo system has verified these are phonies. They aren't the deceased's photos by visual check and by facial ID. They will end up boarding the flight at Gate B5 at 1250 hours. We've got 30 minutes to boarding time. Got your San Antonio, Terminal B screen up?"

"Yes, up and ready to go," Kelly said.

Kelly and Carrie had become the team others studied for airport gate post-screening five-minute drills.

"You take the right side food court after screening," Carrie replied. "I've got left side coffee stands, bar, and ATM. Then let's continue, you watch right cameras, I'll stay on left side up to their Gate B5. Let's watch each side of Starbucks for them coming out right or left if one of them ducks in there to stay out of sight of the cameras.

Carrie had connected them to the San Antonio Airport's Emergency Unit's communication system.

"The two special takedown agents are walking into the food court now," said Carrie. "San Antonio team, this is Carrie and Kelly from NOIHMLA unit. Verify ID please?"

"Rawhide here. I'm in adobe-colored shirt by Sbarro," he said in a hushed voice.

"Sunflower here. I'm in light blue pant suit by ATM," she whispered.

"Got you both and verified with facial ID. Do you have the two passports of the Ghosts on your mobiles?"

"Affirmative," they both said.

"Folks, I've got Ghost One walking toward the men's restroom across from Gate B3," said Carrie.

"See the target," said Sunflower. "He's all wrong. Has worn-looking slacks but brand new shiny brown slip-ons. Must have gotten his others dirty on his trip here."

"Ghost Two is on other side coming toward restroom outside B4 for American Airlines," said Kelly. "Same bright new brown slip-on loafers with faded jeans. Doesn't fit and staying on other side away from United gate for now."

"Got him in sight," said Rawhide. "I'm going up to the newsstand on the side toward Starbucks. Sunflower, you'll call the GO on the takedowns when you see I'm in place for mine."

"Affirmative," said Sunflower.

Carrie and Kelly went silent. They had handed off four minutes after the call to the takedown team.

They watched as Sunflower blended in with passengers walking forward toward B5. Ghost Two had walked out of his restroom on the other side and was pulling his wheeled carry on case. He stopped at the newsstand's right side with Rawhide just around the corner with his back to him reading a magazine from the stand.

"Carrie," whispered Sunflower, "can you get a visual on cell phones in hand for either?"

"Yes, Ghost One is out of restroom and has cell in right hand by his side," said Carrie.

"Ghost Two has his up, seems to be looking for a message or the time," said Kelly.

"Ghost One just pulled his up and is beginning to dial or text," said Sunflower. "Move in. We are GO for take-down, Rawhide!"

It went down like two quick, awkward dances.

Sunflower, a blonde, smiled as she walked toward Ghost One when he stopped on the left side of the newsstand. Momentarily distracted from his mobile phone, he was in her quick grasp. The wrenching of his right wrist caught him by surprise. She quickly pivoted him around, and jammed his hand up behind his back. She took the mobile from his hand as she got ready to cuff him. Ghost One found his nose pressed against an issue of *National Geographic Traveler.*

Around the corner of the newsstand, Rawhide had put his magazine back in the rack, curled out quietly with others walking by on their way toward the restroom Ghost Two had just come from.

Ghost Two was looking at his mobile with a puzzled look on his face when Rawhide suddenly did a downward, clenching grip on both of the Ghost's shoulders and buckled his right knee with a sideways kick from behind. With a quick twirl, the Ghost was pinned to the floor with his left arm wrenched up behind him and Rawhide's left knee on his shoulder and neck holding him down. He quickly grabbed the target's mobile lying on the floor, examined it and pocketed it.

Four transportation officers had joined to help. Two were carefully examining the Ghosts' carry-on luggage.

Passengers in the immediate area watched with quiet alarm but everyone stayed where they were as the professional takedowns looked like an improvised slam dance and MMA event on opposite sides of the newsstand.

"Targets neutralized," said Sunflower. "Burner cells in hand. Escorting out of terminal."

Ten minutes later, they called in that both targets had a new, light density plastic explosive that escaped detection on the luggage screening machines. Twenty minutes later their fingerprints came back from an Interpol list of known North African-trained terrorists who'd disappeared from their tracking the previous year.

"Good job, Carrie," said Sunflower. "How did you know these were phonies with dead Texans' names? We don't even have those deceased lists."

"New test software of filed death certificates from states compiled within a month after death," said Carrie. "It was Kelly's idea to compile it and call them Ghosts. Good one for the team today."

"Good to be part of this team today," said Rawhide. "You detected one we'd never have known about if they'd ignited by the newsstand or on the flight to D.C."

"You two have beers on the Riverwalk, on us, when you get down here, okay?" said Sunflower.

"Make mine wine and we're on," said Kelly.

"Okay, enough dancing in the end zone here," laughed Carrie. "We're back to the salt mines."

Several minutes later, Kelly walked to the back of Carrie's desk.

"I think I've earned a break." Kelly said in a light voice.

Carrie turned around and looked at Kelly's drawn expression. She was leaning against the credenza behind Carrie.

"That was tense," said Kelly with her palm up, shaking slightly.

"I know. It was dicey," Carrie said as she met Kelly's look.

She switched her desk and Kelly's to the remote coverage group.

"Let's take a R & R break."

◆◆◆

Carrie and Kelly, along with "Sunflower" and "Rawhide" later got Unit Team Citations. Kelly and Carrie were both grateful for the internal recognition and honor. But it sometimes was twice as draining to have such a great, emotional, tense save for national security…and have to go home and never talk about it with anyone outside the unit. Ever.

♦ ♦ ♦

Kelly and Carrie went to the exercise track above the unit's gym up on 2nd floor. After they both walked for 30 minutes, Carrie returned to her station. Kelly stood behind Carrie's desk, spending the last 30 minutes of the break watching the cable news channels for the "reclassified news" as Carrie and she sometimes jokingly called it.

"Who you reviewing to finish the day?" asked Kelly when they finished their R & R break.

"Ruth's the passenger who is going to be asked to make an involuntary visit with our counselor for DPC in Denver," said Carrie. "That's the third time in three trips through O'Hare that she's either yelled, slapped their wand away, or what she did today. She kicked the poor agent who did her wand job special and professionally. Time for some *Disruptive Passenger Counseling* in Denver.

"And Anita, she's our next GABA. She's been there three years and is still rude to anyone who asks a question after she gives the 'Prepare for our search and conveyor system' speech. She delivers it in her speed demon, monotonous voice. Most people can't even catch what she says.

"She's had a verbal and written warning. She's good on the technical part of the job but she's stuck in a rut with an indifferent attitude that embarrasses the rest of the crew. Time for Barry and some *Gate Agent Behavior Adjustment* counseling. He's our 'saver' at O'Hare," said Carrie as she pointed at his picture on the monitor.

"Hey, he's cute and about the right age for one of The Trinkets," said Kelly. The Trinkets were their nickname for two system analysts they knew from national security classes.

"No, let's spare him," Carrie laughed. "Why would I try to set up one of our contract clinical psychologists with someone who watches the Astrology Network for dating and nutrition advice?"

Kelly laughed as she wound down. "Which ones are you monitoring now?"

"JFK, Charlotte, and Las Vegas," said Carrie. "Remember coming back from your bachelorette party in Vegas? If I was a terrorist looking for a soft target, I'd be an Elvis and slip in line with the hung over bachelorettes."

"They could have done it with us," laughed Kelly. "We were wasted and that Elvis was old enough to be my dad. He was still pissed they took away his cane at the gate."

"Well, they don't have any flagged travelers there today," said Carrie. "Charlotte and JFK are okay, too. So far."

"Any threats on the news and entertainment front?" Kelly needled as she looked up at the large screens of cable and network news.

"Yeah, looks like one of the chit chat teams is doing their afternoon ritual of bi-polar analysis," said

Carrie as she looked up for a few seconds. "I swear, they'd get fired if they approached an issue as having a third view."

Carrie switched on her ditzy voice. "Hey Wayne, can I try door number three for an original thought?"

She switched to her mock baritone, "No, Boa Feather Brains, you'll get fired if you don't stick with our bi-polar two door approach to issues, honey."

Kelly yelped as she burned herself from her spilled coffee. As usual, it was from laughing at one of Carrie's shots at the media.

"I swear, if part of the viewers had the chance, they'd sue some of them for malpractice," Carrie said as she continued to review Dallas/Ft. Worth, JFK, and then back to O'Hare on her desk screens.

Carrie kept her eyes on Charlotte gates.

"Come with me so I can get a quick coffee too, okay?"

They came back from coffee and looked up at the cable news flat screens.

"Oh, good. It's time for our Celebrity Trash News update." Carrie's sarcasm was dripping now.

"Hey, the reality show mom got new implants for her boobs. Well, that's hard news."

She loved these private breaks as much as Kelly did. It was therapeutic since she couldn't picket a TV network with a rude sign outside the show's window.

"Oh, oh." Carrie was in full mimicry. "He's out

of celebrity rehab! That oughta be worth a talk show or two before his next movie is out."

She leaned back in her chair, savoring her coffee and verbal destruction of celebrities.

"Are you done, Joan of Arc?" Kelly laughed as she shook her head.

Carrie sat a few seconds scanning Dallas/Ft Worth and JFK. She looked up at Kelly from her console.

"The presidents, the circus parade from Congress, and the Super PACs are unmanageables. They are their own huge dysfunctional car wreck. But so many in the electronic media insult our intelligence on a daily basis. *Right or left.*

"They've had a roll in this slide into polarization. They are partly to blame and they know it. They are enablers in this sick process.

"Too many are biased, smug, aloof, and in denial about their role and behavior," said Carrie angrily. "They're often lazy on issue research that's never been easier with Google and a brain. This bi-polar analysis that fits their network, cable news, or legacy newspaper's agenda is infuriating.

"And their arrogance! When they present what they purport to be a verbatim leak as accurate and true when we know differently from inside."

Kelly gave a firm nod of agreement.

"It's not my folks' Buick. It ain't Cronkite anymore. Their profession is polling at or below

Congress. That puts them just a few notches above animal abusers."

"Carrie!" Kelly whispered. "Don't say it so loudly. Someone might hear you!"

Carrie lowered her voice, speaking to Kelly with her head lowered behind her screens.

"Leaks are going to happen. And some of those leaks are healthy sunshine. There IS too much over-classification that's CYA, not for national security. But the opportunistic leaks are escalating and we know so many are not accurate," said Carrie. "If the public only knew how often the leak is meant to help the party leaking it or hurt their adversary. A lot of these are not for the good of the country, just the leaker's agenda."

"Time and again, the media, right to left, let the American public down on a covenant to cover all sides of an issue in a full, fair, and objective way," Carrie said as she looked back at the airport security screens.

"I fear for the republic."

2

Numbland Security

"BS. HE WAS not checking me out!" said Carrie. "I was standing by the Captain Morgan."

Kelly nearly tipped off her bar stool, laughing. Carrie snorted as she reached over to steady Kelly.

Carrie's kitchen counter was covered with Chinese takeout boxes. They were nearly done with the third bottle of wine.

"Which one is this one?" Kelly said, holding up the bottle.

"It's the pink Moscato. The flirty one," Carrie said. "Like you! Asking him all about the differences of this new wine line."

"I was not," said Kelly. "Well, maybe just a little. It's been a year. John seems to look at me like a late model Chevy now. I used to feel like a BMW when we first started dating."

"Yes ma'am, this Riesling is like you, a radiant in our line," said Carrie in a lame baritone voice. "And you should sample our pinot grigio, a bright. And the un-oaked chardonnay, a fresh."

Carrie gave her friend a sly grin. "Fresh all right. He got you to buy one of each. Four bottles! I was afraid you were going to run off with the wine man!"

Carrie stopped, and pulled the fourth wine bottle in front of her. "Thanks for talking me into leaving work after exercising," said Carrie. "Then coming home with take-out for winos."

"Speak for yourself," laughed Kelly. "I was an informed, sophisticated wino…I mean wine connoisseur, tonight."

"This has been a good night," said Carrie. "Let's clean this up, throw away the evidence, and let John pick you up."

"Noooo Sireee, Mom," said Kelly. "We've got one more bottle. Let's talk some more and finish it off in the living room."

"Mom? You lippy punk," Carrie said in mock indignance. Kelly was three years younger and teased Carrie about watching out for her like a mother.

"We're fine," said Kelly. "John said we'd cross that bridge when we came to it. I think we're all happy tonight."

"Did you get to talk to Jeff?" asked Kelly as they cleaned up.

"No, we haven't talked for two weeks," Carrie said flatly. "He couldn't get to the secure Skype. He always wants to know what I'm doing. Doesn't want to talk about how he really is when I ask."

Carrie and Kelly walked over and plopped down on the sofa with the last bottle in tow. "Okay, let's finish this puppy off," said Carrie.

"Now, isn't this better than this afternoon when you said you 'feared for the republic?'" asked Kelly.

"Okay, okay. I was having a drama queen moment." Carrie let out a sigh. "Sometimes I just get numb with all of this."

"Well, yeah, you work longer hours than anyone, managers included. You have a lot of pressure, you have to make tough calls at work. And Jeff. That adds up. Anyone would get numb."

Carrie shook her head. "No, it's not about work. Yeah, I do stay too long, too often, but I'm making a *difference* in a critical way. We stopped terrorists with the new plastic explosives this morning. *We saved people*.

"No, it's about feeling numb, going to Numbland. A few years ago I needed to escape. Jeff was over there again. It all just got too overwhelming. I'd drink two or three of these alone. Several nights a week," Carrie held up the bottle.

"These last 10 years of war," said Carrie. "The

mass shootings at schools, churches, synagogues, workplaces. At shopping centers, theatres, and military bases. A lot of people just need a place to go for Numbland.

"Remember when NOIHMLA was formed last year?" asked Carrie. "I told you later that my secret handle for it would be Numbland Security."

Kelly nodded. "I still think it's funny but noooo, I won't let anybody else know."

"I know," said Carrie. "But for me, it has two separate meanings. One is our nickname for work. The other is life."

Carrie leaned back into the sofa and looked at the ceiling.

"Numbland Security is where we go for peace for the soul, to find strength, to escape, withdraw, to cope and, hopefully…to feel secure. We go there when we're numb from what's going on in our country, in the world," said Carrie.

"Numbland can be a place where we go for safe harbors, escapes that can be good; some can be bad. Some are therapeutic; some destructive, some counterproductive," said Carrie.

"I'm sorry," said Kelly, "but that's kind of dark."

"Hold on." Carrie looked back at Kelly with her hand up. "I think some of the places we go when we're numb are good.

"When I say safe harbors, I mean things that saved me. Family, religion, spirituality, exercise, reading, music, community, and friends that count." She gestured toward Kelly. "People, belief in a higher power, and friends who are there when you need them.

"And thank God for food," Carrie continued. "There's a safe harbor! A warm bowl of soup on a cold day, apple pie, ice cream. Yeah, even bacon and eggs."

Kelly laughed. "Yeah, I overdosed on ice cream and candy bars when John didn't call me back for a month. It was after that first romantic date on a Potomac dinner cruise. Then he's AWOL! Come to find out he'd punctured his groin on a pole on the golf course. He was too scared to call me. To tell me! Then the stitches healed. The doc told him he was still a stud. He finally called!"

They both laughed again.

"And some of the numblands are bad," said Carrie. "Crazy escape sex, binge drinking, and road rage driving. Add street drugs and prescription drug addictions. Bad harbors for escape.

"Some escapes on the home front are safe," continued Carrie. "Family, running, walking, and exercising. TV, cable, or satellite."

Carrie paused and scanned the ceiling, almost forgetting that Kelly was there. "Soaps, Hallmark channel, DIY, HSN, and food channels. Guys go to ESPN, military/history channels, and old Western reruns."

Carrie's eyes were at half-mast. She went on, speech a little slurred. "The Internet wasn't there 25 years ago. Facebook. Instagram. Twitter."

She paused. "The Internet can be a dark hole for the soul."

Carrie barely noticed when Kelly got up and went to the bathroom.

When she came back, Kelly squeezed Carrie's shoulder as she sat down. "I got it, Carrie. Sometimes I park in several of those dark holes."

"We live in a world hungry for hope," said Carrie. "We need to learn to disagree without being dismissive."

"I love you for that," said Kelly. "After everything you've been through, you always come back to hope."

They were both quiet for a few moments.

"I called John," said Kelly. "He asked if I'm driving home. NO! Can Carrie give you a ride home? NO! Carrie and I were both falling off our stools in the kitchen. I've got a cab coming. Here in 15 minutes. John's already home. He was soooo sweet! He even said he'd drive me to work tomorrow." Kelly yawned. "You give me a ride here after work for my car?"

"Roger that," said Carrie with her mock salute. She slid down to the floor next to the sofa.

Kelly sat next to her. "I'm sorry. I'm sorry you're going through this."

There was an uncomfortable silence for several seconds.

"Hey! A drink to something special!" said Kelly with a flourish. She held up her half-filled plastic cup of wine.

"Haven't we been doing that all night?" snorted Carrie.

"You saved my ass!" exclaimed Kelly as she tapped her glass against Carrie's. "I was going to quit last year. I hated Monty Thaxter, the Third Turd." They laughed at Kelly's secret name for him. "I didn't see any way out with him as boss."

"He was a power hungry jerk, trying to use our information access to blackmail like J. Edgar," said Carrie. "And so incompetent."

"He got the job through connections, not merit," said Kelly. "Hell, he made me sign him into the network each morning!

"If you hadn't written that white paper about cutting down on embarrassing YouTube posts and streamlining airport security, they'd *never* have created NOIHMLA. We're in an *accidental* new department because the oversight committee and the White House wanted the bad PR on YouTube to go away."

"Yeah. Who'd a thunk it?" said Carrie. "With all of the growth of NI/TIC, we got to work in a new organization."

"That was accidentally started, *by you*. And I got to come along," said Kelly.

"Yes! Life in Numbland can be bizarre at times," laughed Carrie as she leaned back against Kelly.

Kelly's phone rang. Cab was downstairs. Carrie walked her down to the door.

"Thanks, Carrie," said Kelly.

"No, *thank you*. I had a great night," said Carrie as she hugged Kelly. "I've laughed more tonight than I have…for months. Love you. See you tomorrow."

"Hope this isn't the wine guy moonlighting as a cabbie," joked Kelly over her shoulder.

For once she got in the last laugh.

3

The River Crossing

MARCH 2011

HE'D FLOWN INTO Winnipeg two days before. It was 2:30 a.m. as they came out of the Canadian woods after a grueling two-hour trek through the snow, bramble, and tall grass. It was 10 degrees with a north wind.

His guide had on night vision goggles over his ski mask. They were several miles upstream from Baudette, Minnesota on the Ontario side of the Rainy River. They walked through the underbrush on the short bank along the river. With a half-moon, they could see the long slim neck that stretched out into the river, nearly to the US side.

The guide slowly scanned the opposite bank, then turned and looked at his "delivery." He reached into his coat, pulled out a pistol, and said, "You'll pay $500 more for these goggles or you won't get to the highway in time for the pick-up."

"I already paid you $5,000!" the other man seethed.

"And you'll pay me $500 more now," said the guide coldly, gun pointed at his chest.

"The Delivery" pulled out his passport sleeve and slapped $500 USD in the guide's hand.

He was nearly to the end of the small neck curling out into the river. He looked back to see if the guide was still there.

You asshole.

Back on the bank, he could see the guide with another pair of night vision goggles on his head. The gun was still pointed at him.

He turned back, walked ahead, holding his canvas bag and backpack above his head. He walked out onto the ice on the river. He shuffled slowly, then increased his speed as he got near the four-foot tall bank on the other side.

Just ahead, he could see a dark spot in the ice, right next to the bank. He veered left toward snow-covered ice. As he stepped forward, the ice suddenly cracked under him. He frantically threw the backpack and bag upward onto the bank as he fell through the ice, waist deep in bone chilling water. He grabbed a tree root sticking out of the bank and pulled himself up out of the water and along the bank until he could get up.

His feet were getting numb. He frantically checked for the backpack. Shivering, he zipped it open carefully. It was still intact. He picked it up along with the canvas bag, and limped away from the river.

He didn't see or know he had been photographed by an infrared camera pointed at the riverbank. It was camouflaged as a limb on a tree 30 feet from the shore. It was one of 15 new sites along the Rainy on the US side. His facial ID would be stored on a new database for the Border Patrol, ICE, and others to scan.

Ten minutes later, he took out his red laser light, flashed it slowly three times, then two quick bursts toward the car parked across Highway 172. It pulled forward, he ran across the highway, tossed the bag in, and laid the backpack carefully on the backseat.

◆◆◆

SOUTH MINNEAPOLIS

It was 10:00 a.m. She was surprised at the loud knock. Her friend wasn't coming over until 11:00 for their daily tea. She opened the door and looked in horror. It was him.

"Thought you'd never see me again, eh?" he said. "Where's my little girl you took from me?"

◆◆◆

"Carrie, we've got a slow-walking 'crier' with a suspicious backpack." It was Minneapolis-St. Paul International (MSP) Airport Security Command.

"She just boarded the incoming tram below and looks suspicious. She's Caucasian, crying, has on a parka like others, but it's too bulky for her size. She's walking slowly, no luggage, just has the backpack on."

"Pulling up your monitors," Carrie said as she connected Kelly to join the line. "Where is she now?"

"She should be arriving on the tram at Level T in 10-20 seconds," said MSP Command.

"Kelly, I'm pulling up live facial ID check from MSP. You on monitors?"

"Yes," Kelly said. "See her on tram exit at Level T. I'll get this ID. I'm pulling up no flys, visa overstays, and related for the incoming protocol."

"Okay," Carrie said. "Got it. Plug it in for intercepts. I'll keep tracking. Yes, she's crying, looking down occasionally but not avoiding cameras. She's really distraught. Good call for Code Red."

"MSP, can you scramble 'The Conways' and 'The Dirty Harrys' to Level 2 of Terminal 1?"

"Yes, scrambling both," said MSP.

"MSP," Carrie paused. "Activate two hot bug drones and coordinate with 'The Harrys.' That's one tango, one foxtrot on the drones. Confirm, please."

"Confirmed," replied MSP. "Will activate and direct one tango hot bug drone and one foxtrot hot bug drone."

Kelly cut in. "Her facial ID is not on the no fly list. Hold on. Here she is on visa overstays. Last name Ziad. She came to south Minneapolis on a six-month visitor's visa two years ago with her three-year-old girl, overstayed the visa, and hasn't come in for hearings. I'm posting for you and MSP Security."

"Got her visa picture for facial ID up," said Carrie.

Down below the airport terminal, other passengers just off the tram jostled for position in line.

Ziad was halfway back in line from the tram waiting to go up the escalator.

"Send this visa picture to your Conways' and Harrys' mobile phones and a separate freeze of her face and outfit as she got off tram, ASAP," said Carrie. "Please have your Harrys check in with names and outfits for themselves."

"We're online," a male voice said quietly. "Snowdog here. I'm the 'Harry.' On Level 2 behind info stand. Navy blue blazer with blue checked oxford shirt and beige Dockers, 50-ish, grey hair."

"Confirmed. I see you, Snowdog," said Carrie.

"Sunbird here," a female voice said quietly. "I'm the 'Harriet,' 30 ft. to left of top of the escalator by stairway door. In a dark blue pantsuit, light blue blouse with red polka dotted scarf. Early 40's, blonde hair."

"Confirmed. I see you, Sunbird," said Carrie.

Kelly interrupted. "Folks, I think I've found why she's crying. Her ex-husband, Ziad, is from the UK.

Changed his name from Campbell after being converted in UK prison. I think he's fully radicalized. He flew from London to Winnipeg two days ago. Entered US crossing river near Baudette at 2:45 a.m. this morning.

"Carrie, I recommend we close in on her. I think she may be crying as a forced suicide with backpack because her ex may be back at her last known apartment address, threatening to kill her daughter if she doesn't do this. He was back in prison for domestic violence when she was able to get a visa to escape from him to Canada," said Kelly.

"First, have The Conways ready to hold up the line and have The Harrys close in for appraisal on Ms. Ziad.

"Two, hover the bug drones near the ceiling above Ziad for possible strikes.

"Three, recommend you send police & SWAT unit to her last known address for possible kidnapping/hostage situation."

There was a short silence on the line.

"I agree," said Carrie. "Implement all that Kelly recommends. MSP, you're on the ground. This is now your call."

Suddenly the tracking monitor changed. Ms. Ziad appeared on the screen of Level 1, on the up escalator on way to Ticketing on Level 2. She was halfway up the escalator.

"Agree with all recommendations. Repeat, agree

with all recommendations," said MSP Security loudly. "Snowdog and Sunbird, let us know when you see her. We'll get The Conways out in front of her. We will commence calling the suspect target Zulu."

Above Level 2, the bug drones hovered. None of the passengers or airlines staff knew.

"Carrie, any more recommends?" asked MSP command.

"Yes," said Carrie. "Cue up Celine's program song overhead and run the decibel levels on your orders.

"MSP Security command, we are handing off to you but will stay online if needed."

"Affirmative," said MSP command. "We have command of tactical."

Carrie and Kelly watched their screens anxiously from their offices as it unfolded. The screen showed a more composed Ziad walking off the top of the escalator. She stopped to look right toward the north security checkpoint, then left toward the south security checkpoint. She slowly turned left.

"Conways south," said MSP command. "Do you see Zulu?"

"C-One, yes."

"C-Two, yes."

"C-Four, yes."

Two seconds later, "C-Three here, yes."

Sunbird started walking in a parallel path toward

Ziad, as if going to the escalator to meet someone. Ziad did not notice her as she walked toward the south side, veering toward the two lines furthest to the right ahead of her. The third line over to the left had fewer people.

"Conways, move ahead to all three lines south, now."

Behind Ziad, Sunbird had pivoted and was calmly but quickly catching up to her with one man between them. Snowdog had covered the distance with quick, long strides that looked like he was just another passenger late for a flight. Both of them had a two-wheeled carry-on gliding behind them.

Slowly but steadily, four people with two-wheeled carts emerged from off camera. Two of them, looking like solo passengers, came from the dining area shuffling slowly. Two more, also walking separately, came slowly from the restroom area.

Like a practiced choreography, three of them ended up four to five people ahead of whichever of the two lines they'd noticed Ziad heading toward. The fourth one went slightly faster to the far left small line that now had others following him…to try to get through the line with the fewest people.

MSP has taken the Conways to a level I never thought of when we set this up, thought Carrie.

"Because You Loved Me" by Celine Dion was on the speakers overhead before Carrie realized it on her earphones. "Music up slowly from 40 decibels to 50," said MSP command. "Sunbird, report what you see on Zulu."

"Backpack looks like it has tight bottom frame, looks soft or hollow on top," said Sunbird. "She has reached into her right pocket twice, now has it in there again."

"Snowdog, report," MSP command said.

"I'm in line to her right," Snowdog said quietly while pretending to talk on his cell phone. "She's pulled her hand out of her pocket again. The detonation chord just dropped down over her front beltline. She's probably got the cord to the backpack going inside her coat around her waist to the trigger in her right pocket. Push the music up, bring Tango down to 10 feet above Zulu. Have Foxtrot hover above it, just in case."

"Music up to 60 quicker," said MSP command.

Ziad looked left and right. She was now about 15 people back in the long middle line amongst three lines of about 50 people in a 10-foot radius around her.

As the music got louder, no one heard or saw the small "insect" drone that looked like a wasp until it landed on top of Ziad's backpack.

Suddenly, Celine Dion's rising voice hitting the high note in the middle of the song spiked from 60 to 120 decibels.

Instinctively, Ziad took her hands out of her

pockets and slapped them over her ears like everyone else. In that second, the insect drone was already airborne, back behind her shoulder. Sunbird had quickly pulled the man holding his ears behind Ziad to the left and out of the line.

The music lowered to 90 decibels. As Ziad looked up to see what had happened to make the music so chaotic, she lowered her hands.

"STING on Zulu. Sting," MSP command barked.

As Ziad's hand was still lowered by her shoulder, the hovering Tango sped forward directly onto her right hand for the sting, then was right back in the air.

Ziad's face wrenched in pain. Her left hand reached over reflexively to hold her right hand, now down on her right thigh.

The song on the loudspeaker suddenly shot up to 120 decibels again. With hands on their ears again, few people noticed or cared as Sunbird quickly stepped up, kicked Ziad's right knee from behind, and followed her down to one knee as she grabbed Ziad's right hand with her own right in a powerful grip.

Snowdog had covered the distance to their line in two long steps and quickly secured his hand on Ziad's right pocket's entrance while holding her backpack upright. Sunbird looked up. Snowdog nodded quickly.

"WE'RE UP," Sunbird said in a firm voice. "Get the elevator."

The song on the loudspeaker suddenly shot back down to 50 decibels and a relieved crowd in the terminal laughed, griped, swore, and went back to putting up with the wait in the lines. They didn't notice another Harry fluidly grab Snowdog's two-wheeler and then glide over to take Snowbird's cart. He pivoted and headed back out of line as if he'd realized he was in the wrong terminal.

Carrie and Kelly watched as few people saw or thought much about the nice woman in an airline uniform and a concerned man helping a distraught lady over to get first aid for her hurt hand. They walked Ziad over to the elevator door that opened with another "Harriett" inside. They walked in and the door closed.

Out of the three lines, one by one, four seemingly tired or frustrated older passengers shuffled out of the security waiting lines. They went off in four different directions to a restroom, a dining room, the down escalator, and the last shuffled over to catch the next elevator down. The Conways were leaving.

Overhead, Celine was ending the song with her finale, singing about *being everything she was because someone loved her*.

◆◆◆

Kelly came around the corner, went past Carrie's door, and kept walking.

"SWAT took Ziad, the dad, down and saved the child," said Carrie, walking out of the office to catch

Kelly. "I've switched both of our calls and coverage forward to the backup teams. We're off for a four-hour break."

"Good," said Kelly over her shoulder as she quickened her pace to the restroom.

Carrie soon followed. When she got in, Kelly was throwing up in the back stall. Carrie went in the next stall, closed the door, and sat down. She looked blankly at the stall door.

We stopped one again. We saved lives but this is taking a toll. I'm too numb to even throw up.

◆ ◆ ◆

They had finished a 10-minute jog on the NOIHMLA track above the gym, and had slowed to power walking. It had become their practice for winding down after takedowns. Every day was stressful to work on the gate monitoring and overrides. The alerts, surprise drills, or real terrorist attempts took their toll for all of the staff in NOIHMLA.

But Kelly and Carrie had become the go-to team for takedowns. For both, it was an adrenaline-rush while they were on, followed by the frightening life or death event live on screen once they passed control to the airport team. Then, the draining relief when it ended. The vast majority had been successful and so far, The Harrys hadn't had to do a kill, bodily or with a Foxtrot bug drone.

And no one outside could know any of it.

"How did you know about Ziad crossing at Baudette?" asked Carrie, still breathing hard. "Where did you find him?"

"His passport came up as a possible person of interest from our names linkage. Listed as probably radicalized in UK prison. He's an orphaned Brit. Petty thief. Lived in North London until they divorced two years ago. Then I suddenly remembered the new border picture stations feeding the databases. He came up as unknown facial ID on one of the trees west of Baudette this morning. We didn't have an intercept match because he wasn't on the no fly list. But it matched the Ziad passport linkage on next cross check."

"Great linkage," huffed Carrie as she looked over at Kelly. "And gutsy call."

"Thanks, it was a first with that new border facial database but it just seemed right. But when did we get The Harrys and Harriets at these airports?" asked Kelly. "I thought they were only at the top 10 traffic airports."

"Added 11-20 largest last month," said Carrie. "Sunbird is a former 82nd Airborne medic. Her son is in Afghanistan. She said she was going nuts at home. She sees this as an outlet," Carrie laughed as she looked at Kelly. "And she plays poker with some of the boys in The Conways in the command lounge."

"No wonder," giggled Kelly. "She did her takedown of Ziad like a pro."

"What about Snowdog? Quick on his feet and still kind of a stud for a guy in his 50's."

"Kelly, you bad girl," Carrie said in mock disgust. "He's 65, an ex-Seal, and bored too. I hear some of The Conway girls got him to join their bridge club."

Kelly chuckled. "What happened to the profile name, 'The Slow Pokes'?"

"It's still called that officially," said Carrie. "But it got nicknamed The Conways when we went to the oversight committee to get the demo group approved as a full program. The vice-chair asked me to be more specific than Slow Pokes. What were some of their traits for slowing down the lines to deter a potential terrorist we've identified.

"I told them I used to watch reruns of *The Carol Burnett Show* with my mom," Carrie continued. "She used to love it when Tim Conway came out as the shuffling old man. Then I blurted out, 'That's what we really need, those Conways.' Slow to take off their shoes, shuffling when necessary, etc."

Kelly threw her head back, laughed, and clapped her hands. "What did the vice chair say?"

"They were all laughing," Carrie said over her shoulder as Kelly caught up. "That was the end of questions. She moved for unanimous approval and I was outta there."

Carrie stopped and they both leaned on the rail of the track.

"What was it like when they used the first Tango to sting the one trying to get through the Miami airport?" asked Kelly.

"Not good. We were lucky," said Carrie. "He didn't drop his pack right away because they had only given him a glancing blow with the bug drone. They learned they had to stop using simulators and have real subjects for practice. They switched the practice bug drones to adrenaline sting instead of the high levels of Sting-Kill when zapping the volunteers from the academies."

"These weaponized insect drones scare me. I hope we don't have to use a Foxtrot bug drone on someone when we're on a live takedown," said Kelly.

"Me either," said Carrie.

They were watching two guys from another unit playing ball below.

"You know, NOIHMLA and our partners have to be responsible with this meta-data access and the power it gives us," said Carrie. "We can't get arrogant or content with ourselves. We can do a million things right and no one will ever know. But all we have to do is one thing wrong, lots of people die, and it will be our heads rolling. The honchos upstairs will skate and blame us for over-reach that they were not aware of at the time."

Kelly looked at Carrie. She nodded with a tired look and went back to watching the pick-up game below.

"I love doing these with you but they are taking a toll," Kelly said before she could catch herself. She looked back at Carrie.

"Carrie, I'm so sorry. I don't know where my head is! You two have gone through more grief and loss than I can imagine."

"It's okay," Carrie said quietly. "It is what it is and I have to live with it. And I have to live without him way too often."

Kelly turned to Carrie, reached over, and hugged her.

Below, one of the guys shooting baskets threw the ball back up toward half court. The other pretended to start a fast break to the other end…as if nothing was happening above.

◆◆◆

CATHERINE KRAKKERS
TWO DAYS LATER

"There you are," said Carrie. "How did you get past the security officers without a boarding pass?"

She was looking at Midwest airport video archives from the past three years of a woman in her 60's who looked like a quiet granny just trying to move through a big airport.

Carrie watched the video replays in amazement as the crafty dodger always picked a busy officer or airline gate agents, then slipped past them behind one or more passengers. She also smoothly dipped under the barrier cord, walked casually outside it, and then came back inside the barrier cords after evading the guards. Then, incredibly, here she was boarding the shuttle bus later for an international flight to London. When they landed, they realized at customs that she had no boarding pass or passport.

The woman had been convicted of misdemeanors for criminal trespassing many times in US airports after charges for felony counts of theft had been dropped…numerous times. Several judges and her public defenders had contended that she had mental health problems, thus should not be prosecuted or held. She would often be released…and found trying to board flights again in a few days.

One judge had derided her for her actions and said she should realize these airlines could have her thrown in prison.

"I don't think they would, do you?" Catherine Krakkers replied. "Imagine what poor public relations that would be for a big airline to do that to a quiet, small woman."

"Oh, boy," Carrie chuckled. "She's been playing all of us like a fiddle. We can't let this cycle go on."

◆◆◆

THREE MONTHS LATER

"Who's that on your laptop?" Kelly asked as she pointed at the woman on the screen. "A new terrorist?"

"No, it's Catherine Krakkers," said Carrie. "She's from the Midwest. I found her after she showed up on the O'Hare airport arrests list several months ago. She was just listed as a 'trespass arrest.' It just didn't fit. I pulled her up and found she'd already had several other arrests with charges dropped or reduced in over 10 airports around the country.

"She's been sneaking past gate agents, airport officials, shuttle bus drivers, and airline flight boarding gates. She evades all of them for what she told the judge were her 'airport adventures all over America'...*with no boarding pass, tickets or passport!*

Carrie went back to scanning Denver gates and said, "We're hiring her as a National Security Specialist."

Kelly choked on her coffee "You hired her as a Specialist?

"Yes, she's a GS-5, like the Quality Assurance Specialists," said Carrie as she left Denver for Portland.

"I assigned Catherine to Barry, NOIHMLA's top contract clinical psychologist in Chicago," Carrie said. "In the past, he's been our best contract clinical psychologist for counseling of wayward passengers and gate agents. But now we've put him in a new position finding other possible means and methods for terrorists trying to get through US airports.

"Catherine and Barry meet twice a month in a

small private dining room at O'Hare. They have Starbucks and Cinnabon, because those are two of Catherine's 'favorites from America's airports.'"

"So Barry's her handler?" asked Kelly.

Carrie was now on to the Newark gates. "No, he's the *International Security Officer in Charge.*"

"We don't have that as a job description," said Kelly. "Besides, what's he in charge of?"

"Keeping track of Cathy Krakkers," Carrie said dryly, then took a long swig of her coffee.

"Look, Kelly, we put the cartel's bankers in Witness Protection. We pay blackmailed spies. And we let terrorists go lighter if they spill.

"Why not get a person who needs some help off the street, stop her escapades from showing up on cable news, and keep the terrorists from having a playbook on how to get through US airports?

"We need to find out from an expert how she deals with our 'gate safety issues.' We're going to give her two free trips a year, escorted by someone from NOIHMLA, anywhere in the US. She's perfect for NOIHMLA's Fitless Protection Program with the other misfits."

Kelly rubbed her temples with her eyes half closed. "Who is going to be her NOIHMLA escort?"

"Barry," said Carrie as she watched La Guardia gates. "He's not happy about it but we told him he has to take one for the national security team. Besides, she's kind of got a crush on him."

"Carrie, Cathy Krakkers has a misdemeanor rap sheet a mile long," said Kelly, looking down at Carrie's laptop. "And several of the judges have recommended her for mental health therapy with her need for attention as she evades detection."

Carrie looked up at Kelly. "Well, if she's crazy like a fox, we need her in our den."

4

Milo Pangloss

APRIL 2011

SHE WAS IN early as usual. "Man, I'm glad this wasn't on my shift," said Carrie under her breath. It was appalling, scary and, in some ways, entertaining.

She was briefed by one of the night shift technicians. They knew they should have watched the security video monitors on multiple screens rotating through the night. They were on the back up desks. And like every shift, they hoped that something didn't happen on one of the 15 small screens they had stacked on their desk system. Hangar 57 was at a nearby DC-area airport that was one of the top-secret security sites they also monitored along with airport security gates.

Carrie began reviewing security tapes of the incidences. 12:35 a.m., early this morning, Hangar

57 security tape: A young white male, the terrorist suspect, had breached the airport's security gates and fences. He had been found in a high security, top-secret Federal joint counter-terrorism unit hangar. Over in a corner, on one of the federal executive jets, someone was heard laughing and jumping. When the security guards had turned on all of the hangar lights, there he was, jumping up and down trampoline-style on the lightweight carbon-fiber wing tip. He was finishing a butt drop against the upswept wing end and returning to his feet off balance when one of the security guards yelled, "HALT, or I'll shoot!"

The young man, in a jacket, jeans and new Nikes with yellow blotches, fell down on all fours on the wing, then slowly pushed himself up to kneeling with his hands up. He burped and said, "You've got me, Sheriff."

As the two security guards continued yelling while they ran forward toward opposite sides of the plane, one tripped on a cable. The other dropped his machine gun as he slipped on the slick concrete hangar floor.

The young man started giggling. He got down on all fours again and crawled toward the jet's fuselage.

"I'm comin,' I'm comin,' guys," the suspect wheezed. As he got to the fuselage, he climbed up on it and scooted himself forward toward the nose with his legs hanging over the top of the Gulfstream. As he gave another pull to scoot farther forward, he rammed against the plane's shark fin-like radio antenna made of slick, but hard, composite materials. As his groin slammed against it, he leaned sideways, groaning in pain, and slowly slid off the left side. He hit the hangar floor 12 feet below with a hard thud, then more groaning. As he rolled over holding his groin, the guard coming around the wing noticed three brown stains on his left chest area where he'd evidently fallen.

Jack, the other guard yelled, "Stay down, you fucker. Bill, I think he's got a suicide vest on under his jacket!"

Bill, now fully in control of his weapon, pointed it at the groaning suspect lying on the hangar floor and said, "I'll cover him. You check for the explosives. There may be a hand plunger."

"Why me?" Jack asked. "You finished basic, you know more about this."

"I'll keep him still, you search him with the butt of your gun," said Bill. "Okay, fella. You stay dead still. We're going to search you."

Bill got up within 10 feet with his gun on the suspect, who had rolled over flat on his back, with his hands up above his head. He was still in pain, in some kind of a stupor.

"Now open his jacket top slowly and look at what type of explosives they are," said Bill.

Jack slowly curled the jacket front back and saw an inside vest pocket. "I can see the three brown explosives. They seemed to have sweated. Maybe dynamite." He jabbed his AR-15 into the suspect's chest and yelled, "Okay. Two questions. Two quick answers or you're dead," said Jack. "Where is your detonator and what type of explosive do you have?"

The suspect just lay there. His eyes were bloodshot and half-closed. "No det cord," the suspect slurred.

Jack slammed his AR-15 into the guy's chest yelling, "Don't fuck with me! Don't use that slang. No 'det' you asshole." He swung the AR-15 across the suspect's face. There was a loud thunk as the butt hit right below the left eye. The suspect was thrown and rolled sideways onto his stomach.

"Shit, don't kill him. We're already in a world of hurt," hissed Bill, barely audible on the video replay Carrie was watching. He reached down, grabbed the suspect by the shoulder, and rolled him back over. His left eye was puffy, his left cheekbone off-center and bleeding from a gash. "You dumb shit, Jack. Get the fuck back," he said as he yanked Jack up from his crouch over the terrorist suspect.

"Okay, listen. I'm going to slowly open your jacket," said Bill. The suspect lay still, moaning and breathing heavily with both empty hands spread out on the floor.

As Bill opened the jacket very slowly, he first saw the three brown stains on the inside pocket of the white liner of the jacket. Then he smelled it. "Is that Mexican food?"

"Yeah," the suspect slurred. "Burritos…the food court."

"Three burritos. The food court! In the airport waiting area! How the hell did you get out of the flight gate waiting area, through security fences and into here?" asked Bill.

"Popsicle sticks."

◆◆◆

When Carrie had gotten in early that morning, it was being handled as a "focused" terror alert. It was restricted now to the top brass and the staff of its joint missions group. There was a Federal requirement that any breach of a top-secret facility or guarded area for plane or vehicle had to be reported to its Director. Directors of the FBI, DEA, etc. *Had to be reported.*

This was an FPE site. It had *Fleet Protocol Exemption* to be at a public or private airport rather than a military airport like Andrews or Dover. The executive jet fleet in the hangar was used as an emergency mission pool by NOIHMLA , FBI, DEA, DHS, and a few other designated agencies.

The problem with this embarrassing episode was that it was not only supposed to be highly secure, it was supposed to be unknown to many members of the appropriate Congressional oversight committees of the growing NI/TIC sites, fleets, anti-terror equipment and spending. The heads of the top-secret clique knew it was occasionally used by directors, executives, and even a chair of one of the Congressional oversight committees…for their first class, personal use. So they were trying to keep a lid on how this suspected terrorist had gotten this far. *They all wanted this to just go away.*

Carrie's role, responsibility, and authority in NOIHMLA was well established by now. She was to do her own investigation, including her own interviewing, review of videotapes—in this case, one of the rare top secret hangars located on the grounds of a public airport. She was required to report her independent findings and a yes or no recommendation for "override" of the existing unit's bureaucracy. If there was a terrorist incident involved in this breach, the normal priority at the site of a breach or incident was for the brass above her to cover it up, not necessarily to make the country safe from another incident of the same type and style.

NOIHMLA was not popular with some of its affected agencies and the bureaucracy they represented. It had override authority, which galled them. And, that override for terrorism meant not waiting months or years for an Inspector General's report. As one of the Senators said in a closed-door Intelligence Committee hearing, "We want to stop hearing from the IG that our horse was stolen a year ago from the barn…and that Osama's son had ridden him out."

Carrie was now watching the 1:45 a.m. video

replay. Two DEA agents had gotten there first after the alert was sent out by the two security guards. They started the interrogation immediately. They decided to run a "field interrogation" using their undercover names. They were talking to him with his hands duct-taped behind his back, sitting on a cheap white plastic chair by the small side entrance door. They replaced the tape with their professional plastic zip tie.

"Okay, listen, fella. The cavalry's here. We're just going to let those guys simmer down and we'll talk with you," said the stocky, short Hispanic agent waving his hands toward Jack and Bill. They were standing nervously against the wall. "Now, where did you come from, and how did you get in here?"

Before the suspect could reply, the tall agent with the beard and scruffy hair stepped in front of the other agent and said, "Enough of that, El Jefe." Leaning down in the suspect's bruised, trembling face, he yelled, "Who are you with?! You better TELL me before the goons get here or you're going to be toast!"

"Milo. Milo Pangloss," the suspect said in agony, looking down. His left eye was swollen shut and his gash had been covered with a small bandage from the emergency kit in the hangar. It was blood-soaked.

"Hold it, Rocco," said El Jefe. "His billfold is still in his back pocket. Damn it, these yokels were more interested in taping him up than finding out if he had ID." He opened it up, pulled out the driver's license. It was a military ID. He looked back at the two security guards, then back to Rocco.

"This is going to be a shit storm," said El Jefe.

♦ ♦ ♦

Who was the suspected "terrorist"? During the interrogation, the DEA agents discovered that he was Private Milo Pangloss, a new 11 X-Ray Infantry grad from Ft. Benning, GA. His blood alcohol level was .30 when they tested him 30 minutes later. He shouldn't have been able to walk, much less climb onto a Gulfstream wing and use it for a trampoline. How the hell had he gotten to this fenced-off part of the airport, gotten in there, past the security guards, and onto the wing?

Milo told them he had gotten very drunk in the airport bar on the B concourse with his two friends from Benning. They were homeward bound on leave but wanted to have one last day and night together after months of basic and AIT infantry. All three were headed for different assignments, so they wanted to have one last hurrah together.

They had spent the day before in D.C. walking the mall from the Lincoln Memorial past the Vietnam, Korean, and World War II memorials, and then to the Smithsonian. Milo's two friends had earlier flights but Milo's was delayed by a maintenance problem. He'd found out after 10:00 p.m. that he wouldn't be leaving until the next morning at 6:00 a.m. He'd decided to drink some more and get burritos before their food stand closed, go to the bathroom, then go sleep on the lounge chairs at Gate B23.

And that's where Milo's memory had ended during his interrogation.

Carrie found a tape of the concourse near B23. "Yup, there you are, Milo. Leaning a little to starboard, young man." He'd stopped, leaned against the wall outside the men's restroom, pulled the three burritos out of the sack, and stashed them inside his jacket. "Yeah, Milo, wouldn't wanna' drop them in the urinal," Carrie laughed. She was growing attached to him. "Enough of that! Stay professional. No sympathizing with terrorists," she said as she took a short sip of her coffee.

Time to find out how he did it. All involved in the interrogations had *demanded to know how he had breached top-secret security.*

Milo had no idea. He was too drunk to remember...then or later. He was now in a private, well-guarded room at Walter Reed. He had five stitches to close up his gash and would have his broken cheekbone operated on in about two weeks when the swelling went down. Milo wasn't viewed as a flight risk or going against medical advice. They were guarding him to keep others from finding out the suspect's story.

Carrie continued her video reviews. 11:04 p.m.

security tape of Gate B24. It was often used by a regional commuter airline that had an outside stairway for passenger loading on the tarmac. Out of the right side of the screen came a still-weaving Milo. He was headed toward the outside door. And it opened! He looked down at something below the door.

It was supposed to be locked. Carrie did an immediate rewind to 10:45 p.m. She did a fast-forward. At 10:55, a maintenance man and woman walked up to the door. He punched the security keyboard, opened the door for her, went outside, then quickly put what looked like a popsicle stick in the bottom of the door jam. It was not completely closed. For some reason, there was no flashing light for an open door on the keypad. But when Milo opened the door and staggered through, it closed completely.

Carrie switched to the exterior video camera on Gate B24. 10:55.

The couple had come out and the man turned to secure the popsicle stick under the door.

"Out for a smoke, are we?" said Carrie in her Church Lady voice. "I think not."

They could be seen going over to a baggage cart train, and heading toward a cart at the back. It had a quilted buffer blanket used for scratch prevention laying on its floor. The lady jumped in and the man quickly pulled closed the webbing-lined vinyl curtains on each side as he quickly took a last look around.

Soon, the baggage cart was rocking back and forth.

"Well, are they checking for missing luggage," said Carrie as Church Lady, "or fornicating like horny little monkeys?"

Next, Milo staggered down the staircase at the left of the video screen. As he regained his bearings at the bottom of the staircase, he was looking at the baggage cart tractor.

"Oh boy," said Carrie as she watched Milo climb on the baggage cart tractor. Despite his drunken state, he seemed to be familiar enough with the tractor to look around a few seconds, push the starter button, put it into gear, and take off with a wild lurch. As he wheeled the accelerating six-cart train around the front wheel of the commuter jet at Gate B-24, the vinyl curtain on the back cart came open with a man holding on frantically while it curled around under the nose of the plane.

Carrie stifled a laugh. "Well isn't that special? Going for a ride on the love train."

Carrie quickly switched to Gate B25. There was Milo's train going 25-30 mph. It was headed underneath a Boeing Triple Seven, between the front nose wheel and back wing wheels. He weaved between wheels as he went under the plane.

She switched to Gate B26 video. As the luggage train started to turn back from under the next Boeing Triple Seven at B26, the last cart's curtain was opened wider this time. Both the man and woman were crouched inside, seeming to be ready to jump out on the run. But Milo, enjoying his new road race course, had cranked it hard left just as he came past the back wheels of the plane. He was only about five feet from the closest tire and each baggage car was coming closer to the wheel as it followed the train's left turn. The lady had lost her balance and slid out of the cart as it was correcting. Her feet were dragging on the tarmac. The video was silent but Carrie could see (and feel) the woman screaming as the man desperately pulled her back in just before the last three of the six carts approached the wheel.

Carrie cringed. As the last cart went past the wing wheel, its body hit the side of the tall wheel. Luckily, it ricocheted sideways to the right rather than bounce upward. The couple could be seen laying inside the car, holding on to each other for dear life. The last cart caused a slight fish tailing of the train but Milo was oblivious. When he came to open tarmac, he slowed, then put on his brakes, coming to a skidding stop.

Milo laid his head sideways down on the wheel for a few seconds. Then he threw up most of a pepperoni pizza on his shoes and the cab's floor. As he regained his bearings, Carrie saw the curtain open slowly on the last cart. They were both looking out, each putting one leg out on the tarmac.

"Run you little sinners, run," Carrie snickered.

The couple took off running across the tarmac back toward Gate B24. The man was zipping up, the woman buttoning up her work blouse on the run.

"Well, well," Carrie said, shaking her head. "We've got some explaining to do about the popsicle stick and door, don't we now."

Milo, relieved of his pizza, had taken off at high speed with the luggage train out onto the tarmac. Out toward taxiing planes.

Carrie's report would later note that for the next 65 minutes, they did not have a video track of Milo's journey after he disappeared out of Gate B24's video feed. Two flights reported that they had to do emergency aborts because of an errant luggage tractor and train running across their runway. The control tower reported seeing the second instance after hearing about the first one from an air traffic controller. Milo may have been out on the runway approaches, on the grass, on a takeoff runway, or countless other places during those 65 minutes.

Her report showed that the airport had full *live* video surveillance of all the airport's gates, approaches, taxi areas, and runways. However, it had *recorded* videos on only 75% of the gates, 50% of the runways, and 25% of the hangar exteriors. Milo had managed to weave off into spaces where they couldn't find him on video recording until they found his hijacked tractor inside the top-secret security hangars area. The tractor had a drain culvert grate bent on its front bumper where he had smashed it against the foundation of Hanger 56 next door at 12:25 a.m.

Milo had taken the train into a 15' by 15' runway drainage culvert that was open on the commercial side but had a drain grate on the restricted area side. Evidently, Milo hadn't quite made a hard right in the grass to avoid the hangar, skidded at an angle into the side of the hangar and flew off the tractor onto the grass. He wandered around the front and could last be seen coming out of the dark five minutes later as he stumbled toward the side door of Hangar 57 that had a sliver of light shining out. Carrie watched as Milo got into Hangar 57 from…a popsicle stick holding it open for smoke breaks.

"Like a moth to a flame, here comes Milo, the terrorist," Carrie shook her head as she stopped the tape review.

Carrie wrote up her recommendations that afternoon:

> *Deal immediately with Hangar 57's security and its less than professional security officers.*
>
> *Get full video exterior coverage of the whole airport. Audit all external doors and their keypads for bypasses.*
>
> *Fire or discipline the two maintenance*

staff and find out who gave the access number to go out.

Look at policy and practices on all luggage tractors' ignition keys or lack of them.

Talk with the airport's security director.

Check on Private Milo Pangloss' Army record to date. If he had no previous discipline actions, consider no charges or Article 15 to avoid an embarrassing JAG question about the "potential terrorist incident" that was averted.

The outcomes from Carrie's recommendations:

- Hangar 57's security firm had their contract cancelled the next day. It was a "security specialty firm" coincidentally owned by the brother-in-law of one of the intel committee's chairs. They found he had a number of security officers who were fraudulently listed as "fully qualified," yet they lacked previous successful law enforcement experience or military police service with honorable discharges. Several had not passed top secret background checks successfully. The two on duty for that Sunday night's graveyard shift

were both listed as "security check pending" the night of Milo's breach.
- A gate agent/baggage handler with an Oxycontin addiction was fired for sharing the code with the maintenance staffer in exchange for 50 OxyContin pills that he supplied his friend every month for a discount.
- The man from maintenance was charged with violation of the FAA gate door requirements and then turned over to local law enforcement for sale of a schedule two controlled substance.
- The airport's security director received a verbal warning that didn't appear in his employee file.
- Private Milo Pangloss did not receive any civilian or military charges. He was told in a one-hour briefing attended by his Ft. Bragg DI at Walter Reed before he was discharged that he was "subject to federal prison time" if he ever discussed or divulged any of the details of this violation of FAA, DEA, FBI, and federal laws. If he did divulge or disclose, he would receive a dishonorable discharge before serving time.

Private Milo Pangloss would head back quietly to a DC airport in late April with an extended leave to make up for his 21 days of "security recovery" at Walter Reed from a "training accident." And, he was ordered to go on his original deployment orders. To Afghanistan…21 days late.

◆◆◆

Later, Carrie went down to the restroom. She slapped cold water on her face and dried it. She looked up in the mirror at her eyes. They were red with dark circles around them.

I obsess about saving us from terrorists. I just laughed at a drunken GI as he cluelessly made a joke of our airport security systems…and I'm terrified every day I'll get that phone call.

How did I get here?

5

Outpost Jackson Afghanistan

MAY 2011

"INCOMING CAPTAIN!" YELLED Franks. Jeff jumped out of his bunk, grabbed his helmet, M-4, and scrambled out the door just as the two mortars exploded by the west wall next to a Humvee.

He sprinted the 50 feet to the bunker. He had 10 feet left to duck his tall frame into the entryway when the gas can next to the Humvee exploded. He felt the hot blast and shrapnel flying around him as he dove into the bunker.

First Sergeant Andy Franks was just ahead of him. Jeff knelt with his M-40 cradled against his gut, then sat down next to Franks against one wall. They watched in the near darkness as three more figures from a nearby squad made it in before the next four mortars exploded.

In the dark, they heard Private Francis and a new voice along with the whine of Lucky, the OP's dog. "Walton, just sit on the floor next to Lucky," said Francis. "Put your helmet on straight…and next time, bring your body armor."

"Sorry," said Walton, the new replacement. "I was worried about Lucky getting out with us."

In the dark they could hear whispering, and the dog soon quieted. "You named him right," Walton whispered. "He's lucky he got out of the mortar, safe in here."

"Hell, no," sniffed Francis's familiar voice. "I named him Lucky because now he eats better than any of us. He gets treats we won't share with each other."

Snickering and groans could be heard in the dark.

Jeff and Franks both laughed quietly with the rest. They sat several more minutes, waiting.

"Six mortars, two tubes, and they're already running back up the gulley," said Sergeant Franks. "Chicken shits, hit and run is driving our guys nuts," he added under his breath to Jeff.

Out of the dark came a familiar voice.

"You know, being in here sometimes feels like having a rubber with a hole in it. It gives you a false sense of security while you're getting screwed."

Jeff and Franks both laughed quietly while the others cackled or slugged Private Francis.

They were deep in Kandahar Province above the

Lowy Mandah River Valley at Outpost Jackson. Captain Jeff Hanford and First Sergeant Andy Franks (Top) had been together for 11 months now on a 12-month deployment to Outpost Jackson. It was set to end in late May…*if* the Afghan Surge ended as they were told.

By now, Jeff and Top could finish each other's sentences and suggest things the other was already thinking about. They both had an unspoken contempt for the choice of this plateau for an outpost, but would not show it to their men.

Like Alexander the Great and others going back over two thousand years, the Taliban came here to the southern crossroads of the Kandahar to start their takeover of Afghanistan. The joint companies of Canadian and US soldiers before them were determined to get a victory over the Taliban strong hold of tribes in the region. A tribal chieftain came to them and said he needed safety from a rival chieftain's group who he said was friendly to the Taliban. That joint force had the Taliban's chieftain killed.

Captain Jeff Hanford's platoon had arrived to find the rival chieftain, with his power consolidated over the other tribe, now a Taliban ally. In the words of one of their Iraq war veteran sergeants, "Time to embrace the suck."

In the 11 months there, his platoon of 50 ground troops had seen 3 killed, 10 medevaced out for surgery or treatment from snipers, IEDs, or mortar attacks. In addition to the 10 medevaced Purple Hearts, another 13 had gashes and lacerations from shrapnel wounds that earned them Purple Hearts, too. Sergeant Franks and Captain Hanford had made sure their unit got the recognition they deserved from the hell they were in at OP Jackson.

Their unit took fire two to four times a day. That often included the terrifying night mortar attacks that brought those who could sleep out of their bunks to one of the four bunkers. They were officially named Outpost Zulu by the joint forces, but was now solely a US OP. Several of the men in Jeff's platoon had wanted Headquarters to rename it Outpost Jackson in honor of one of their medics, Specialist Freddie Jackson. He had been killed just a month into their deployment during a night mortar attack. He was dragging one of the injured soldiers to the east bunker. Jackson was hit in the head below his ear by mortar shrapnel just as he was getting into the shelter behind the injured soldier he'd saved.

HQ wouldn't change the name. So the soldiers, amongst themselves, called it OP Jackson. Hanford and Franks used Zulu for reports but called it OP Jackson at daily formation. Morale at the OP was more important.

Outpost Jackson was on a flat plateau 700 feet above the Lowy Mandah River but still lower than a mountain top two miles behind them. At night, the

Taliban would sneak along below the edge of the plateau ridge out of sight of their night scopes and mortar them. Jeff led a squad to put in unattended ground sensors (BUGS) listening devices in the gully on a day patrol. The Taliban had the nearby village kids come and take them out that afternoon.

The next week, a night patrol was sent out to put in more BUGS, but the Taliban had night vision goggles they'd taken from dead soldiers and equipment truck convoy ambushes. Their forward observers used them now to take out the new BUGS at night.

The next night, Jeff used the last resort. He hated it. Another gully in Afghanistan had land mines in it. He was haunted by their patrols going through villages and seeing legless and armless children from over 30 years of war with Soviets, Taliban, and now the NATO alliance.

◆ ◆ ◆

Earlier that day, Captain Hanford had done his daily report and an update on supplies they'd get the next day from Kandahar base camp. "Men, we're still going to patrol, sometimes even nights to keep the enemy off balance. We're not going to sit still for a siege and roll up in a corner." He finished and said, "Top, do you have anything else to add?"

"Yes, sir," said First Sergeant Franks. "Guys, these are your brothers. This is your family. We stick together and watch out for each other. If someone gets that 'thousand-yard stare' when their eyes look like the pilot light is out, let somebody know, so we can talk. Let me know. We'll stick together to finish this. We've lost guys. We've had badly wounded. You will never forget them. We will never forget them. We'll get out of here because we're together and we trust each other with our lives. We'll get out of here for ourselves and for them."

Franks looked at Jeff.

"Dismissed," said Jeff

◆◆◆

They were back in their hooch after the mortar attacks.

"I heard a couple of them talking about how many days are left tomorrow as they walked away from the bunker," said Franks. "I'm just going to leave them alone about 'day counting' as long as I'm far enough away. I'm just not going to hear it."

"Agreed," said Jeff. "They're holding on and sticking together. They have each other's backs. That's how we let them survive this."

"Sir, you've got blood on the right side of your ass," said Franks, pointing at a three-inch blood spot on his rump.

Jeff stood up, pulled his waistband down in the back, and wiped off the blood. It was just a bleeding slit.

"NO ONE hears shit about this, Franks. It's just a slit of shrapnel in my ass. That is NOT a Purple

Heart. Got it? You're the medic tonight. Go get some damn tweezers," said Jeff angrily.

"Yes, sir," said Franks as he gave Jeff a grin. "Won't be on the morning report."

Franks got the tweezers, wet wipes, and a bandage from the kit. He gave the half-inch long red slit a few smears, gently pushed in with the tweezers, and dug it out.

Jeff gritted his teeth but didn't flinch.

Franks pulled it up to look at the fingernail-sized piece of metal by his lamp light and tossed it in Jeff's canteen cup. He put a butterfly bandage on the slit, then followed with a large bandage over it.

"Field surgery over, Captain," smirked Franks. "I'll send you my bill later."

Jeff popped the back of his long johns back up, looked at Franks.

"This is so fucked," said Jeff, shaking his head.

"It is. Let's get the rest of these guys out of here in one piece."

They both got in their bunks.

Franks turned out the lamp.

They lay quiet for a few seconds.

"How many is that for you, sir?" asked Franks.

"Two from first tour, one on the second," said Jeff. "And none to report this tour, asshole. How about you?"

"Two that I counted on first tour, one big one on my second tour from the IED that flipped our

Humvee, and then the five stitches on my shoulder from that sniper shot our first month here. Lucky so far too."

They lay still in the dark for a minute.

"Night, Franks."

"Night, Rockhead."

Jeff chuckled. "Okay, had that one coming since you got to see some ass."

Jeff pulled his body armor up on him. During the cold nights at this OP, most of the guys slept with their body armor as a safety cover before they put their blankets on.

For Jeff, it was sentimental besides.

Jeff reached for his cell phone. He couldn't, and didn't use it for calls out at their OP. They had to use the secure Skype in the commo shack.

He opened it up to his pictures. To Carrie.

My brown-eyed girl.

He put in the earphones and turned on his play selection. Early in the deployment, he'd stopped playing this song because it had become too emotional, too hard. But for the last month, he often played it because it helped him finally fall asleep after weeks of stress and insomnia.

Someone Like You started. He was back in another time, when they would get lost together.

She was in his arms, alone on their own dance floor by an old dresser in her bedroom as the CD played this song.

Before he'd become cynical and depressed about endless war over here and increasing sadness back home for her.

Before he'd turned angry and hard inside. He'd been young, free, and had faith in the future.

He tapped the body armor on his left chest. Under the Kevlar of his older, lighter ceramic armor, it was there. On the left breastplate, it had "Love you, Carrie" written with black marker.

Each time he had gone on a foot patrol, a mission in a Humvee, or made it through another IED explosion, Jeff would gently rub his plate over the heart in gratitude for being alive, in one piece.

She's saved me from myself, so many times.
29 days.

6

Tall, Beautiful, and Dangerous

JANUARY 2000

"OKAY, GRUNT, BACK to the grind," said Dave. The icy Midwestern wind stung their faces with loose snow from the weekend snowstorm. "Y2K didn't crash the grid. Freeman State's back in session for the new millennium."

"I never thought I'd yearn for Ft. Bragg's summer heat, but I'm starting to now," said Jeff. "I'm glad I got the one weekend leave last fall. It was great to get back here and see Amy."

"Hey, Jeff, look over at Fleener Hall," Dave said. "The tall one in the parka."

"Yeah, she's tall all right. Has hiking boots on," said Jeff. "She could probably look down at you and say 'Gimme 20 push-ups. Just for being short.'"

"Screw you, Hanford. I'm 5'10," said Dave. "I'll

call you Lurch like Drill Sergeant Meadows did in class if you start that shit. He didn't like your 6'4" ugly face. I enjoyed every push up you got from him."

Jeff's eyes were still on the tall girl. Then it hit him. "It's her," said Jeff.

"Who?"

"Station. The volleyball star," said Jeff.

Carrie Station tossed her parka top back and was shaking her long brown ponytail as she walked in the door and stomped her feet.

"Man, she's not just tall, she's good looking," said Dave.

Jeff nodded.

It's a new millennium. A guy can look.

"Yeah. I saw her play the Saturday I was here in October. She was Freshman of the Year last year. She spiked a ball so hard for game point, the back line just ducked it. She's the whole package."

"Yeah. Tall, beautiful, and dangerous," said Dave. "Don't let one of Amy's spies see you looking at another girl."

I treat Amy like a princess. Looking doesn't mean she's off her pedestal.

"Nah. And don't let on that I know who Station is if she's in our history class," said Jeff. "I love to play with their mind if they have a big head."

As they walked in the door and out of the wind, Dave said, "Knock yourself out, Hanford. She could probably kick your ass and take names."

As he walked into class, Jeff saw her in the back of the second row. He walked to the back of the third row.

Think I'll have some fun on my first day back.

"Man, that wind bites," said Jeff as he swung his backpack down.

"Yeah," said Carrie with a slight smile. "Pretty arctic out there today."

"You a history major?" said Jeff. "I was gone first semester and am still catching up with folks."

"No. I'm a computer information sciences major," said Carrie. "Taking an elective. But I like history."

"Computer sciences?" said Jeff. "Do they make you carry your own floppy disks and mouse to each class?"

"No, that would be the engineering majors," said Carrie, rolling her eyes. "Some of us are working on website security and the wireless world of the future."

Whoa, slow down. She's sharp.

"How about you?" she asked. "History major back from a semester off after spring break in Florida? Livin' La Vida Loca?"

Jeff paused and looked at Carrie. "I wish," he said. "Went to basic and transport AIT in the Army for six months. Joined the National Guard last year."

When he mentioned the Army and Guard, the look on her face changed. "I'm Carrie. Carrie Station," she said, looking him straight in the eyes.

God, those are beautiful brown eyes.

"Jeff Hanford, sophomore plus. Going pre-law with a geology minor."

She smiled at him, still looking right into his eyes. "Welcome back, soldier," she said.

Jeff was about to thank her when the professor spoke.

"Ladies and gentlemen, let's get the new year, the new decade, the new century, and the new millennium off to a good start," said Professor Franklin Thompson. "This is *United States History since 1877.* If any of you got confused coming across the tundra today, time to pack up and find where that other course is located.

"I see some familiar and new faces," Thompson said over his glasses, looking at Carrie and some others in the class.

"Let's get something clear. If you are majoring in history and *not* planning on teaching, or attending grad or law school…and have a minor in poli sci or geology, you have rocks in your head if you expect to get a job right out of college!" Thompson surveyed the crowd melodramatically, then began calling off names from the class registration list.

"Well, Rockhead, looks like you're set," Carrie whispered to Jeff.

◆◆◆

The next day, Jeff walked into *History of Ancient Rome* early. He looked to the back of the room and saw Carrie.

"Second row, last seat," said Jeff as he walked to the back of the third row. "Is this random, or a seating plan?"

She looked over at him and smiled slightly.

"Just a choice when I'm in an elective and want to stay out of the way as much as I can."

"Yeah, I get the back row, but why not a back corner?" asked Jeff

"I'm computer systems, Rockhead. We do numbers and sequences. We program for the probabilities. Most professors and TAs at least make a lame attempt at surveying all corners of the class. They tend to scan the back left, then quickly skim over to the back right. Or right to left."

She is definitely smart. And, sees things from a different perspective. Refreshing.

"You may be on to something there. I spent six months hiding from drill sergeants in formations trying not to get noticed," he said. "Trying not to get nicknames like Rockhead."

Carrie laughed, then stopped. "So are you recovering from this trauma all right?" Carrie said with a side glance to Jeff. "Does the Guard have support groups for your type?"

Two rows to her left, Dave stifled a laugh.

Jeff felt like reaching over and smacking Dave.

"Good one. Okay. Good one," he said smiling at Carrie. "So why are you going to wade through the Roman Empire if you're just doing electives?"

"Their empire's systems weren't rivaled for another millennium," said Carrie. "Organized government, roads, aqueducts, military and communication way-stations that many of our power grids borrowed conceptually.

"And Roman coins from Spain's mining. You should like that...for geology," Carrie said, giving him a smug look.

"You'll like this class," said Jeff, deciding not to keep up the banter. "I've heard Hansen's more comfortable, not uptight like Thompson. Watch out for Thompson. He's old school and having a hard time dealing with the instant search world. He hates to be corrected with proof.

"Dave had him for Humanities last year," Jeff said, gesturing toward Dave. Thompson said that in some ways, Hitler 'was a young vagabond who jumped at the chance to save his beloved Austria' at the start of World War I.

"A student came back the next day and quoted 'the young vagabond' as one of William L. Shirer's more famous commentaries on Hitler from 'The Rise and Fall of the Third Reich.' The kid was toast for the rest of the semester."

"Well, I won't get on Netscape for quotes tonight," said Carrie. "You do know which one that is, don't you?"

Jeff looked at Carrie, then with a cheesy grin he asked, "Is sarcasm a second language for you or were you born with it?"

Carrie smiled, then turned to Jeff. "Actually, it's brothers. I'm the youngest with two older brothers. I couldn't win many fights so I learned to shoot from the lip early."

"Let me guess. You were Daddy's princess?" Jeff asked.

Carrie blushed, like she was surprised he went there. "No, I can still beat up my brother, Kent, if I feel like it," she said as she returned a cheesy grin to Jeff.

Woman, you are dangerous.

♦♦♦

MARCH 27, 2000

He came in the door, looked back toward her and smiled. She enjoyed seeing his 6'4" 215 lb. frame ambling back into class again. And she couldn't deny she enjoyed those deep blue eyes.

"How was spring break, Carrie?" asked Jeff. They were both getting to Thompson's class early. "Beat your brother up for off-season training?"

"Funny, Rockhead," replied Carrie, returning her gaze to the screen notes up front. She didn't want him to know that she'd actually been looking forward to seeing him again. "You saved that up for a few months, huh?"

"Just making sure you're ready for next season," replied Jeff.

He knows I'm on the volleyball team but he's never brought it up!

"Ladies and gentlemen, today we're going to trace some of the people and forces that shaped the

Prohibition movement," Thompson said as the screen lit up with a dark, angry figure.

"Here's a slide of one of the early 'proponents,' shall we say, of Prohibition," he continued. "That's Carry Nation. All 6 feet of her dreaded, fiery incarnation."

Carrie didn't take her eyes off of the screen. There was Nation in a dark bonnet and black full-length dress. The hatchet held up in her right hand, open Bible in her left. And the grim, determined look.

Shit, Carry Nation again. I had this thrown in my face in high school. Rhymes with you and tall as you.

"She was arrested many times for chopping up saloons with her hatchet," Thompson smirked. "'Hatchetations' she called them. She sometimes greeted men in the bar with a cheery 'Good Morning, Destroyer of Men's Souls,' before busting the place up and heading righteously to jail. Some saloonkeepers had joke signs up saying, 'All nations welcome except Carry.'

"Nation was famous, some say notorious, from the 1880's until her death in 1911. She lost standing even amongst fellow prohibition advocates when she announced that President William McKinley, whom she'd said was another secret drinker, got what he deserved when he was assassinated in 1901."

Thompson mercifully moved on to the Methodist's Women's Christian Temperance Union and the Anti-Saloon League through 1920.

Finally, the class ended. Carrie quietly stashed her notebook in her backpack, got up, and walked up the aisle.

"Hey Carrie." Jeff had caught up to her in the hallway. "I'm going over to have a couple of beers at the Hofhaus. Don't come over and chop the place up with your hatchet."

Carrie flushed. *The six-foot tall crazy woman joke again.*

Tears welled up just as Jeff looked at her. She turned around to walk back the other way.

"Carrie, I was just kidding."

Carrie firmly swung her arm back at him to keep his distance as she walked quickly away.

"Way to go asshole," she heard Dave say as he walked by Jeff.

Jeff didn't get back to his apartment to study after a beer at the Hofhaus. Instead, he spent the rest of the afternoon and evening having more than one.

◆ ◆ ◆

The next day, at 12:53 p.m., Carrie watched Dave walk into class without Jeff. He nodded politely to her, then quietly sat over in his usual fourth row, back seat.

A few minutes later, Jeff walked in. His face was ashen, eyes blood-shot.

He slowly shuffled back and started to say, "Carrie…" in a rough voice when she cut him off.

"Well, good morning, destroyer of men's souls," said Carrie in a cheery voice.

"I had that coming," croaked Jeff.

7

How Harry Won In '48

MARCH 2000

"IN RECENT AMERICAN history, no presidential election was more surprising than Truman's upset win in 1948," said Professor Thompson. "And, I think modern conventional wisdom that the polling in '48 wasn't as sophisticated as our polling today is the main reason Harry won."

"Do you think they have factored in the quiet, secret vote of so many World War II veterans, Professor?" said Carrie. She hadn't raised her hand.

Jeff glanced at the clock. Five minutes left.

"What do you mean, the 'quiet, secret vote,' Mizz. Station?" said the professor as he dragged out the Ms. into a Mizz.

Jeff looked over at Carrie and saw that look in her eyes. She wasn't even slightly intimidated by

Professor Thompson's tone or question. "There were 16 million veterans who served for the US. 300,000 combat deaths, 100,000 more dead in training, transit and all," said Carrie. "So many injured and disabled. But that left 15 million that at least got to come home to live and vote."

"So, back to the question. What makes them a 'secret, quiet' vote, Mizz Station?" replied Thompson, in a slightly aggravated tone.

"Field Experience, Professor."

"Field experience?" said Thompson, now sounding smug. "A great many of them were not on the front in the war, Ms. Station."

"No sir. I meant the history department's Field Experience course," said Carrie. "I did a veteran's history for mine this spring with my Great Uncle Jack, a World War II Navy veteran."

Jeff looked at Carrie. *She's calm and polite. Hell, she has him back-pedaling.*

Thompson, trying to hide his embarrassment over the source of her information, asked with a smug smile, "And what did this ONE interview with one of the 16 million veterans of World War II tell you about the Truman vote surprise in '48?"

Carrie didn't miss a beat. "That you're right about primary sources, sir. We need to get as many as we can to back up what we hypothesize about history." Carrie rolled right on. "He said 'there were millions of us either out in the Pacific or they were on their way over from Europe to join us to invade Japan in the Fall of 1945. And Harry dropped the bombs on Hiroshima and Nagasaki. We got to go home alive because Harry dropped those bombs.'"

Carrie continued. "Uncle Jack's final point was surprising, but I think makes the most sense now about Truman's upset in '48.

"He said, 'Many of us were from Democrat families that didn't like Harry, others were Republicans, and a great many didn't care for any politics at all three years after the war. But Harry dropped the bombs, we got to come home, and we quietly went in and voted for Harry. That's why it was such a surprise.'"

Thompson had gone from smug to miffed, his face turning red. "And how do you think your Uncle Jack can be so sure of that supposition? Veterans were a big part of the population that Gallup polled in '48."

Jeff looked at Carrie, eager to hear her comeback. She didn't disappoint him.

"Uncle Jack said, 'We didn't tell any polls the truth. Hell, we didn't even tell our folks or wives the truth about that vote for years,'" said Carrie.

Several in the class laughed out loud when she quoted her salty Uncle Jack's "supposition."

Thompson was glowering as he came back for one more push back. "And what made you so sure of your Uncle Jack's historical veracity, Ms. Station?"

Several students were visibly aggravated at the insulting style in Thompson's tone.

Somehow, Carrie kept her cool. "The widows, sir," she said. "Several WW II widows asked Uncle Jack if they could come down to hear his video interview in the dining room at the retirement center. He told them they could, but no kissing and cheering on VE Day."

Jeff loved it. Several students were laughing again but everyone was hanging on what Carrie had to say next.

"It was the widows' nods, sir," said Carrie. "Two of the three nodded, the other held her head down. But they all cried as he told the part about not telling their wives."

Carrie sailed on without a pause.

"I think the history department was right to add the growth of oral histories as a means of collecting a more balanced history and additional primary sources. Many of these ground soldiers, sailors, and flyers will never write a memoir on their own. They are valuable first person histories that we're losing every day. They can be asked questions to check their veracity. All good historians should balance these with other sources and our own judgment. The widows were my visual but definite additional sources, sir."

"Interesting. And well presented, Ms. Station," said Thompson in a less-than-sincere voice. "But still, how does that make Truman the upset winner in '48?"

"They didn't have exit polls in '48," Carrie replied. "And, that's if they can be trusted. Angry, alienated or very private voters might not tell the truth, then or now.

"As you said, Truman's upset was a 2.14 million vote margin," said Carrie. "He only needed that margin out of 15 million surviving vets to win. Many were too humbled or embarrassed to say anything about their service for fear of offending the disabled and families that never got to have their loved ones come home. Truman, the accidental president who surprised them with his backbone in '45, saved their lives, as they saw it. 'He saved my life' is one of the most basic reasons anyone could vote for someone in an election, even if they won't admit it. I think it explains the Truman upset, sir."

Thompson was silent for a few seconds. Jeff was half-turned toward Carrie. He started to clap in a quiet, respectful way. And then, several other students did too. Thompson's brown-nosers sat like statues, insecure for their grades and approval.

"Well, good discussion, class," said Thompson finally. As if everyone had just participated in an inconsequential chat. "We'll see how Ike gets America out of Korea on Friday." And he walked out quickly, not staying for the usual questions from the brown-nosers.

Jeff noticed several of the seniors looking over at the sophomore information systems major. Carrie had just politely, but convincingly, humiliated Thompson, and he never saw it coming.

Jeff stood up and looked at Carrie, who had her head down. Her hand trembled as she put her notebook in her backpack.

"Good job, Carrie," said Jeff. "You just changed assumptions on Truman's upset and put an insufferable ass in his place. You probably torpedoed your chance at an A. But good job."

"Well thanks, Rockhead," said Carrie sarcastically as she returned his grin. "I'm so glad you could enjoy it."

Several students had stopped at the top of her row. Jeff held back as they congratulated her. One asked how she could do an oral history to meet her "Field Experience" requirement for graduation next year.

Jeff walked out and waited down the hallway. After Carrie finished talking to the last student, she walked toward Jeff with her bag slung over her shoulder. He uncharacteristically opened the door for her to walk down the stairway.

"To what do I owe this honor, Mr. Hanford?" she said as they walked down the stairs.

"Do yourself and our history department a favor," he said. "Take your minor in history. What you did today was incredible and important.

"We don't need another computer geek with only bits and bytes flowing out of their mind when they finish here," Jeff said. "We need more balanced, down-to-earth thinkers who aren't afraid to buck the conventional wisdom of the high priests in each field. We need leaders like you outside of just the volleyball court." He half expected her to laugh at his little speech.

She looked surprised by what he'd just said. "Oh, so I don't end up just a volleyball playing computer geek after college," she said, smiling at him. "Why should I be a leader outside volleyball and computers, Rockhead?"

"Because our country needs leaders with guts. And you've got guts," he said, pointing at her. "We need leaders who won't send people off into the world…or into wars without thinking outside the box."

Afraid he'd lose an argument too, he didn't wait for her reply. Jeff pivoted and was down the stairs before Carrie could reply.

◆ ◆ ◆

It was the last week before the spring 2000 finals. They got to Thompson's class early, as usual.

"Hey Station," said Jeff. "What's on for your summer?"

"I need some advice, Rockhead. I'm going to go for a minor in history. I want to look at next semester's schedule so I can plan ahead."

He was surprised, but thrilled that she'd actually

taken his advice. "Okay, get a print out of the history minor curriculum and bring it to class Wednesday," he said. "I'll tell you what I know about classes and professors. But you need to make sure you take the courses you'll value. Okay?"

"Deal," said Carrie.

◆◆◆

Later, as class finished, Carrie looked at Jeff.

"So what's on for your summer plans?"

"Well, I've got my two week Guard summer camp commitment in July. Transportation unit training. Then work for a friend of the family's construction company. How about you?"

"I'll work at Fielding's," said Carrie. "It's a great dinner club where a lot of my friends work during the summer when they're back from college. I'll spend a lot of time running and staying in shape for next season too."

"Sounds good," said Jeff.

"Jeff," Carrie said as her look turned serious, "I tease you guys, but I want you to know I admire and appreciate what you and Dave do in the Guard."

"Thanks," said Jeff, surprised. "We don't hear that very often."

"Be safe," she said as she got up to leave.

Dave walked over to them just as Carrie was leaving. Carrie waved bye to Dave and walked out.

Jeff and Dave waited, then walked down the stairs when they were out of ear-shot of the rest.

"If only Amy would tell me that instead of whining about why I ever joined the Guard," said Jeff.

"Sounds like a personal problem, Lurch," said Dave. "Maybe you ought to take it up with the chaplain."

Dave ducked as Jeff swatted at him, then took two steps at a time to the landing. He pivoted, smiled, and sang in a high pitch, "She's gotten under your skin."

Maybe she has.

8

Summer 2000

INTERVALS

"PRIVATE HANFORD, YOU dumb shit! INTERVALS! Keep your fucking INTERVALS!" yelled First Sergeant Florence at Jeff. They had just rolled in from their first 10 miles of the convoy escort field exercise. Florence had run back from the Captain's jeep.

"Yes, First Sergeant. I'll get closer," said Jeff. "Kiss their butt…"

"Kiss their butt?" yelled Florence. "Hanford, it's kiss their bumper for intervals, during urban street run and 300 feet when you're on an interstate or open road like this one. Can you get that!?"

"Yes, sir…I mean, First Sergeant. Kiss their bumper."

"Hanford, you may be a college boy, but you sure

are a shitty driver," Smitty laughed from the shotgun seat.

"Smitty" Barrell Smith on his nametags, had taken basic, then transport advanced training with Jeff the year before. They knew each other but this summer they had been assigned to drive their Humvee together. Jeff enjoyed Smitty but this afternoon, he was pushing it.

"I'm a better driver than this, Smitty." said Jeff. "But I do suck on Humvees for the first couple days. It took me until the second week last year. But remember, I was second on the final driving test."

"Yeah, well some girl or crappy used car has got your head up your ass since then," Smitty said, giving Jeff one final needle. "Let's get out for chow. Top's up there in line and he should be full after chewing your ass."

The rest of the day went better for Jeff. Smitty took his turn for the next 20 miles. He had problems too on intervals on the highway with the heavy, touchy gas pedal. As Smitty liked to joke, "Hanford, I'm from the hood, you're from Franklin. But we *both* are screwed on this Humvee."

When they pulled in for the middle afternoon stop, Florence came strolling back after chewing on the screw-ups. He saved his best for last, Hanford and Smitty.

"Are you two brothers from another mother?" asked Sgt. Florence, looking in Smitty's window.

"You both can't do intervals for shit. Like identical twins."

"I don't know, Sergeant," said Smitty. "You always say, 'Anything's possible in this man's Army!'"

"You think you're funny, Private Smith? You want to do stand-up comedy tonight?" Florence said, just inches from his face. "I can arrange for four hours guard duty instead of the usual one tonight. You like stand-up, Smitty, don't you. Well, we can arrange for you to be funny all night!"

Smitty leaned back and shook his head. "No, Top. I'm serious. I'm going to be better tomorrow. And my man Hanford, he's ready too."

"You better be. This ain't funny, you two," said Florence as he walked away, then he stopped and looked back. They were both holding it in. They knew he'd look back, they'd heard he would. Then he was gone, past the big supply truck in front of them. They both broke out laughing.

Florence was a retiree, a career man, now in the reserves. Not a lifer. The guys respected him. The ones who were squared away loved him. The rest, the newbies like Smitty and Jeff on their first summer camp after basic the year before, were on trial. But like some of the former drill instructors (DIs), Florence could be a stand-up comedian himself...*but you couldn't laugh.*

By Wednesday, Jeff and Smitty were "squared

away" on intervals. Florence slowed on his stroll past their Humvee that day, pretending to be thinking about dropping a reign of scorn on them again. But he didn't, and they spent the next 10 days of their summer drill actually having fun. When they were late after lunch on the first Thursday, Florence had asked, "Where are the twins?" Two guys in the front of the formation started to laugh. Florence had them down doing 20 when Jeff and Smitty showed up.

"Hanford! Smith! Get over here. You're late. Get down and gimme 20! Do you know why your two friends are doing 20?"

Jeff knew better than to answer the rhetorical question.

"They didn't know you two were twins. Brothers by another mother who can't drive for shit when they show up for summer camp!" Jeff could tell that Florence was having a good time now. He would turn around and catch a few more cracking up at Hanford and Smitty, the twins. By the time formation was finished, Florence had 'caught' six more smirking when he got in their face and they did 20.

On the last night, Friday, before they drove back from camp to their home base, Smitty and Jeff found Sgt. Florence coming out of his tent and going over to a picnic table alone as the sun was setting. "Hanford. Smitty. Join me?"

Smitty looked at Jeff, then they both said, "Yes, First Sergeant."

"It's Top tonight. Let's just have a beer before turning in." They talked as the sun set. Twilight came and then the stars came out like you never see in the city. Jeff asked Florence if he'd tell them about where he'd served. They'd never gotten a chance to talk to many of their DI's or training instructors last year.

"I hope things stay like they have recently. We can handle the Kosovos and some of the "peacekeeping missions" but we don't need any more Mogadishus. We've got to have a clear mission and end game like we did in the Gulf War. This man's army had been turned around since Vietnam, but it wasn't when I came in. I didn't have too many good options except drugs, gangs, and eventually jail."

Florence stopped, took a swig from his beer and looked up at the night sky.

"My dad was there but got sick and died when I was in junior high school. I was lucky to have him that long. Most of the guys around me didn't have a dad at home. I swore I'd try to be a dad, like my dad had been. But I got married too young, then got divorced before we had kids. Then I went off to Germany, Korea, and back to the 82nd. That's where I got my CIB for Desert Storm in '91.

"A lot of the Vietnam career guys told us to enjoy it. If there was a parade when we got home, go do it. I did, and remember feeling the pride they showed leading us back in that armory to those bands. On the

Fourth of July, we were invited to march in town in a parade. That was nice."

Dad would have loved talking to Florence, Jeff thought as he continued to swig his beer.

"Then the Soviet Union split up and it looked like we'd have a new world of peace. A few of my friends were in those units in Somalia. One year and seven months after we won the ground war in four days in Kuwait, we lost 19 of ours, two of my friends, in two days there. Part of it was the different administrations and leaders, to be sure. But it was obvious we were in for a long struggle if we got caught up in tribal pissing matches in those areas. I hope you guys don't have to deploy to that.

"That bombing of the embassies in Africa two summers ago bugs me. That Bin Laden guy has a case of the ass for us and we'd better pay attention to not just him but the anger he represents. He doesn't get those guys to go into his training camp in Afghanistan just for summer camp fun."

The nearby camp fire flickered as Florence looked at Smitty, then Jeff.

"Pay attention to that. Just because the Cold War is over doesn't mean we can lull to sleep in this vacuum of the US being the world's only super power."

Florence finished his last beer. Then he shook hands with each of them and said, "This was my last summer camp. I owe the wife and girls my full life now. I won't see you after October weekend camp.

Twenty-four years is enough." With that, he went into his small tent.

Smitty and Jeff walked back along the lane next to the tree-lined woods where they'd bivouacked.

Jeff turned to Smitty, "I wish some of our history professors could make me feel the respect I have for him when he talks about the world."

Smitty gave a thoughtful nod. "I wish I'd had my dad around more...and he'd been more like him."

The next morning, Jeff drove the first 20 miles to a rest/maintenance stop. As they pulled up in line, Florence came back through the line of Humvees and trucks, kicking ass and taking names again like last week. He got to them. He stopped and looked at them both, his hands on his hips. "Wipe those smiles off your faces. You twins can't find your ass with both hands. Get out and give me 20."

◆ ◆ ◆

FIELDING'S

"Two orders up, Carrie!" Roy Fielding announced from the dining room. "We're serving people, not waiting for a serve."

"Yes, Mr. Fielding," Carrie said. "Sorry. I had two wine orders."

"Welcome back," laughed Liz as she whisked past with a tray of food above her head. "He still teases me about Homecoming court."

"He actually enjoys all of us that made it through

the first year," Liz said while they waited for more orders at the window. "He's snippy because Christine missed tonight. She begged for the part-time busing job. Money's probably tight since Zach was born. He's sick tonight and she didn't call a replacement."

"I didn't know she was on for the summer," said Carrie as they both took orders out. "She didn't say anything about it on the phone last week."

◆◆◆

"Oh, he's getting so big!" said Carrie as Christine met her at the front door. Christine was Carrie's best friend in high school. "Can I hold him?"

"All night and tomorrow if you want," Christine laughed as Carrie held her arms out for Zach. He clung to Christine.

"Welcome to my world. He won't go to other women but when Tim's buddies come over for cards, he's their guy. Don't take it personal."

"I'm sorry it's been a few weeks since I could get over," said Carrie. "Roy scheduled me six straight nights my first week and I've been sleeping in and running each day. I know, that's lame compared to your days.

"We missed you at Liz's Memorial Day weekend party. It was most of the old crowd and a few with girlfriends or boyfriends here to 'meet the folks.'" Carrie said with air quotes.

"When are you going to bring one of those by?" teased Christine as she changed Zach on the couch.

"Not this summer," said Carrie. "No boyfriend now, but I'm good.

"I'm glad I dated that basketball center last year. I think it was both of our freshmen flings. But it seemed too casual for him when it was done. Don't get me wrong. It was great to be out on dates with a guy taller than me…with heels! Dinners, movies, and pizza Sunday nights."

"And what about sex?" giggled Christine. "You forgot that part! That's what you talked about at Christmas when you were home." Christine picked up Zach, started for the basement, and pointed to the clothes bucket at the top of the stairs.

Carrie grabbed the bucket and followed her down. "Really? I talked about sleeping with Rick? Sure, it was great to have a boyfriend to have sex with. I didn't remember talking about it so much."

"It was just you and me alone shopping that one day," said Christine. "You were finally having a real relationship that your brother Kent couldn't scare out the driveway if he caught the guy looking at your chest during dinner."

They both laughed.

Carrie looked up. "Yeah, I did finally get to have the full experience. It felt great." She looked down at the basket as Christine had flipped clothes one-handed into the washer, talked, and held Zach on her hip.

"How do you do all this, Christine?" Carrie asked.

"I can hardly balance study, practice, eating, and sleeping a little each day at school. You do a diaper, carry on a conversation, toss in the wash while holding Zach, and I'm just here reminiscing about my first sex life in college."

Christine looked at her and pulled Zach up closer. "That's how, Carrie. He and Tim are my world now.

"The days are long, I'm tired, there isn't enough time for anything," Christine said. "And sex? We'd have to get a sitter and we can't afford one," she laughed. "But I don't regret it. I hope I'll be able to go back to school someday, but this is my life. I love Tim and Zach."

They went back upstairs, got Zach down for his afternoon nap, and went back to the living room.

"Carrie, I'm sorry I couldn't make it to Fielding's last week for busing tables," Christine said as she threw a pillow to the end of the couch and lay down.

"Zach got a fever, threw up, and I couldn't find time to even call the team for a replacement. I called Roy to apologize the next day. We agreed I wasn't ready to come back to that type of schedule. He was really sweet. I'd begged for just those hours in the evenings when Tim could be home. But that night, he was out on an overtime job at the power plant."

"You're doing a lot. Don't sweat the job at Fielding's," said Carrie looking out the window at the neighborhood with small homes, young kids, busy parents, and mini-vans. "I just love Zach. And

Tim's a good guy. You've got a family. It's different."

Carrie looked back. Christine was asleep on the sofa. She pulled the blanket over Christine, kissed her on the forehead and said, "I've got to get home and get ready for Fielding's. See you soon."

Carrie got home, went out running at 2:30, and still pulled into Fielding's by 4:00 for her night shift.

My world's good. I'm not ready for Christine's world.

9

The Reformation

FALL 2000

"HEY, CARRIE. HOW was the summer?" asked Dave as he walked into the first class of *History of the American West.*

"Good," said Carrie. She looked around for Jeff, wondering why he wasn't with Dave. "But I was ready to get back to school after summer with my parents and my brother. How was summer camp?" She really wanted to ask about Jeff to make sure he was coming back this year.

"Good. Better for me than Rockhead. Our first sergeant used to be a drill sergeant. He rode Jeff like a rented mule and it was fun. He did more push-ups the first two days for screwing up intervals than I saw him do in a month in basic."

"What are intervals?" she asked.

"New tactical driving. New book last year, *Black Hawk Down,* is about the Battle of Mogadishu in '93. They had to learn to use closer intervals in their urban combat formations than the usual 300 feet between vehicles in regular road convoys. Now you have to be able to "kiss the bumper" of the one ahead of you at 25-35 mph speeds. It's hard. Jeff's great at it once he gets used to the Humvee's clutch again. Do *not* tell him I told you that, okay?" said Dave. "Here he comes."

Oh boy, he's got a great tan now…and that damn grin. He's filled out more. God, he's more handsome than last winter.

"Well, Ms. Station. What brings you to History of the American West?" Jeff taunted as he strode down her aisle.

Well good, smart ass is back. And loaded for bear.

"I like cowboys," Carrie shot back. "What's your focus? Want to study the rocks they hid behind during shootouts?"

Dave stifled a snort in the next aisle.

"Well, the summer hasn't mellowed your sarcasm," smirked Jeff. "Ready for another season?"

"Of what? Volleyball or retorts with opponents half-equipped for a battle of wits?" said Carrie, as she pulled her book from her backpack. *This is going to be a fun semester.*

◆◆◆

"You're taking *The Renaissance & Reformation*?"

Jeff said to Carrie as he walked into class before Thompson arrived. "Going for big art and violent drama for $1,000, Alex?"

"YES, I'll need to, Rockhead, okay?" snapped Carrie. She wasn't in the mood for his sarcasm at the moment.

"Hey," Jeff said, holding up his hand. "I'm sorry. Sometimes I overdo this."

"Overdo what?" Carrie said as she put her backpack down. "Have a smart ass remark for everything?"

"Wait, what do you mean, 'you'll need to'?" asked Jeff.

"To get all the classes I'll need for this minor in history."

"Well, it's still great that you chose it."

"Yeah, it's really great," she shot back at him. "I didn't see all of this coming last spring. It's going to take nearly two classes a semester the rest of the way."

He looked down at his notebook. "I was serious last spring. We need more people like you who'll challenge the status quo."

Jeff looked at her, his eyes intense. "You took on Thompson last spring.

"And still got an A from that arrogant ass," Jeff added as he gave her the 'grin'.

God, he's aggravating when he does that. "Think I can get the right classes in two years?" she asked.

"Yeah, if you get a good advisor," said Jeff, melodramatically straightening up.

"Good," Carrie said, leaning forward and talking past Jeff. "Dave, you available for advising?"

Dave laughed at Carrie. He looked back past Jeff. "Sorry. My schedule's too full with classes and weekend Guard. How about I appoint my second in command?" he said as he nodded toward a glaring Jeff.

"Ye Gods, Beavis. I'm stuck with Butthead?"

◆ ◆ ◆

A WEEK LATER

"Rockhead, I didn't get to ask you how Guard summer camp went," said Carrie as she packed up her backpack after class.

"Good. We worked on convoy discipline, intervals…complicated tactical maneuvers."

"Oh, like finding your way to the Flamingo Bar in Plainfield on Saturday night?" Carrie shot back.

Jeff glared at Dave, who grabbed his backpack and made a quick getaway.

"No, more complicated than HIS maneuvers," Jeff said shaking his head toward Dave.

She's serious. She's looking at me like she wants to know more.

"Actually, it was good," he said as they took their time walking out. "We had a career NCO, a guy who retired as a sergeant major, as our first sergeant at camp. He was good for all of us. He paired me up with Smitty, a guy from Peoria. Smitty was good to pair with. He could make me laugh even when we were hot, tired, and sweaty.

"We had to learn to be a team in a Humvee with this new concept of '300 feet on the roads, kiss the bumper on fast urban patrols.'"

"So you were Hannibal and Mr. T in your own 'A Team'?" she needled.

"Funny," said Jeff with an irritated look at Carrie. "Did you watch reruns all summer?"

"Actually, it sounds more exciting than running in the morning and waiting tables at Fielding's," Carrie said as she looked directly at Jeff.

"Nothing wrong with good, honest work," Jeff replied as he looked at her. "Like my dad used to say." He looked away as they walked down the stairs of Fleener Hall.

"Your dad 'used to say'?" asked Carrie.

"Yeah, like he used to say."

My God, I haven't quoted Dad for a long time.

Carrie looked down as they walked toward the library, making it easier for him to keep talking.

"Um, my dad died in a car accident right after I'd turned 16."

"Oh Jeff, I'm so sorry."

She's speaking from her heart. Amy never talks like this.

"We'd just had an argument. He told me to be

glad I had a car at 16," said Jeff. "He went on about how he never had one of his own 'til his senior year. I told him I'd paid for half of mine like we'd agreed. Told him to get off his high horse about his day.

"I took off angry in my car. Mom said he left a few minutes later to go over to Grandma Jean's, his mom. She was fighting cancer at the time."

Carrie walked on in silence, giving him the space he needed to keep talking.

"They said he probably never saw it until it hit him. A big truck ran a stoplight and broadsided him. He died instantly."

Carrie stopped.

"I'm so sorry," Carrie said as she put her hand lightly on his arm. "I can't imagine losing my dad like that."

Jeff fought the adrenaline that ran through his body from her hand on his arm.

"Don't get me wrong. My dad, he was the greatest dad. It was one of those normal father/son arguments." Jeff's voice grew quieter. "Just at the wrong time."

Jeff swallowed and looked up at the sky above Fleener Hall.

"I miss him every day. I realized this summer talking with Smitty that Dad's part of the reason I joined the Guard," said Jeff. "Dad was a Vietnam vet, '69 to '70. Mortar man/company clerk on a firebase. Said he was always scared but made sure I knew he was lucky. Didn't have to go on patrol. *Platoon* spooked him. He had nightmares for months but then, just didn't talk about it anymore."

Jeff looked down from his gaze at the roof of Fleener. "Mom and Suzy, my little sister, took it hard, too. Grandma Jean died six months later. The next year was the worst year of my life. First summer, first Fourth of July. All the firsts without my dad. It was hard on my little sister, too. She was just two years younger than me. I quit teasing her then. Sometimes I'd just let her come in my room when I got home and cry. It was the only time I'd cry. Never in public after the funeral. Dad was tougher than that. I had to be tough too."

Jeff looked at Carrie, surprised to see tears running down her cheeks. She looked up at an old elm tree by Fleener, to try to hide her tears.

He wondered if it was a mistake to tell her so much. He'd never meant to make her cry. "Carrie, I'm sorry," he said. "I don't know where that came from. I haven't told anyone here about my dad except Dave. I guess cause you're the first girl I've teased like Suzy…since Dad."

"Well, that explains a lot," choked Carrie, laughing in relief. "I'm the little sister who got baited, teased by my brother, Kent. And he's two years older," she said as she wiped her eyes.

"Yeah, no wonder," said Jeff. He was glad she'd lightened the mood "Except you're taller."

"Thank you for reminding me, Rockhead." Carrie's laughter bubbled out into the fall air.

"You're welcome," said Jeff with a grin as he turned toward the Union.

Man, she's something. Amy and I never talk like this.

◆◆◆

Later that night, Carrie left the library just before midnight and turned toward her dorm. As the sidewalk curved left, the floodlit Campanile came into view. There they were.

It was a custom to kiss the one you loved at the base of the Campanile for all 12 chimes of the bells 100 feet above.

Underneath the Campanile, at the floodlit foundation, five couples kissed as the first chime began.

And there was Jeff kissing Amy. It figured he'd be dating a petite, beautiful blonde.

I hope she knows how lucky she is.

10

Brad

"CARRIE, IT'S BRAD," Erin whispered as she covered Carrie's cell phone speaker. "*Brad Kippick. The star wide receiver. I forgot. Amber said he might call.*"

Not another jock.

Carrie had just gotten out of the shower. "Can it wait?" she asked, throwing on a robe.

"No!" Erin whispered. "Amber told him to call after he asked about you!"

What am I, the spinster sister they have to line up for dates?

"Okay. Tell him I'm coming."

Brad Kippick! The cute, tall, football player who flirted with our table…well, all the tables at the Hofhaus last year.

"Hello, this is Carrie." She hoped he didn't hear the nerves in her voice.

"Hi, Carrie. This is Brad Kippick. I talked with Amber the other day. I hope you don't mind me calling this late on Sunday."

"No, it's fine. I'm getting ready to study a couple more hours."

"Yikes. A scholar."

Ye gods, not another cute, dumb jock.

"Not really. I usually outline my notes to drill it in a bit." Carrie laughed nervously.

"Yeah, uh. I was wondering if you'd like to go out for pizza or a movie?" Brad stammered.

"Well, could it wait until the weekend?"

Erin slammed her hands into the futon frame. Carrie turned around to see her mouthing "NO! You idiot."

"Well, we've got our first game on the road this weekend, so that's not so good," said Brad.

Idiot. You deserve to be a spinster.

"I'm so sorry," gushed Carrie. "I just got out of the shower. I don't know where my head is."

"Really!? I should have come over in person to ask for this date," Brad blurted out.

Carrie laughed before she could catch herself.

He's quick and a rascal.

"No, I think that would be more scary for you than me," she said.

What am I, a 9th grader?

"So how about pizza some night before Friday?" asked Brad.

"Sure, okay. How about Tuesday?"

"Great," said Brad. "How about Tony's? I'll pick you up at your place at 7:00."

"Okay. Let me give you my dorm address."

"That's okay. Got it," said Brad. "Amber gave it to me yesterday. See you Tuesday."

◆ ◆ ◆

"Amber, why didn't you tell me you were lining me up with Brad Kippick!" said Carrie when Amber walked in from her date later that night.

"Why didn't I? Why didn't I?" Amber barked as she tossed her purse down and stomped across the room. "Because you are the saintly sister of the team. That's why. One romance your freshman year and you're sequestered in the library or dorm after classes since then.

"Brad asked me about you last night when he was coming out of the Hofhaus. He said he'd like to meet you and knew I was on the team. That's guy talk for *I want to dump Sarah and go out with Carrie, the hot looking volleyball player*. Comprende?"

"Wait. I'm the 'saintly sister of the team'?"

"Carrie, sit down," said Amber as she put her hand on Carrie's arm. "One of the girls in Accounting class dates Brad's friend. They've gone out. He's no dumb jock. He's funny, maybe even as sarcastic as you if he's pushed. He's smart. Majoring in marketing. He's the 6'5" star wide receiver! Runs like a deer, leaps like a gazelle, makes impossible catches.

"And he wants to date YOU! Got it?"

◆ ◆ ◆

"Carrie, thanks for going out on short notice," said Brad as he opened the door to Tony's.

Eyes turned and looked at them. She was used to being looked at.

She's that tall volleyball player.

Not tonight. As they walked through to a booth near the back, she felt it. The admiring look. She'd given it to others for years but this was a first.

She glanced sideways and saw it in the wall-length mirror above the booths at Tony's.

She and Brad looked like a couple.

Later, when they walked back to her dorm, he asked if she liked karaoke night.

"Well, not as a rule. Some on the volleyball team go there once in a while," she said. "Why?"

"Well, sometimes for a study break, I come down on Wednesday nights for 9:00 karaoke," said Brad. "I'm going tomorrow night. Amber and some of the volleyball team might come. Why don't you go along?"

"Brad Kippick!" Carrie said as she whirled under a street light. "Why is everything lined up between you and Amber? What am I? The spinster, goodwill project for you this fall?"

Brad looked stunned for a few seconds. "No, you're no goodwill project," he calmly said. "I know who you are now. You're the girl who was pretty but too tall to date in high school.

"You're sarcastic because it's a good defense mechanism to keep guys from getting close and hurting you," said Brad. "I doubt you even know how beautiful you are."

Brad put his hands gently on her shoulders. "Okay. Here it is. You're the whole package. You're funny, you're smart, you're a great athlete. People, not just Amber, say you're a big heart behind the stand-off posture. On top of all that, you're beautiful. Drop dead beautiful."

She stood there stunned. Brad pulled himself toward her. She didn't stop him.

He kissed her lightly at first, then gently pulled her into his arms.

A rush went through her body as she held the embrace.

"No one's ever said that to me," she said. She leaned her head into his shoulder to hide tears.

"I imagine so," whispered Brad. "At least I got to be the first one."

◆◆◆

Amber couldn't stop talking once Carrie got back to the dorm, asking about the night, what he said, the kiss.

"On karaoke nights at the Hofhaus," Amber

laughed, "one of Brad's favorite acts is "That Old Time Rock and Roll" and sometimes, "Bohemian Rhapsody," *Wayne's World*-style. Brad sings the lead with friends from the football team joining him. The crowd loves it as Brad and a 230-pound tackle sing the high parts while a junkyard dog linebacker and the center sing the frantic 'back seat chorus' on chairs behind them. Brad and the tackle play Wayne and Garth from the front stools."

Carrie and Erin were giggling with the beers they'd gotten out. Amber was wound up.

"Sarah, his old girlfriend, is fuming. He dumped her last weekend and her girlfriend heard him asking about you after their argument Saturday night. She thought they were on autopilot for Homecoming," laughed Amber.

"She came up to him in the Union on Monday and said something to the effect of, 'You're going out with that tall volleyball chick over me? Well Kippick, you're going to REGRET it!" Amber was doing a screechy voice as she finished. Carrie and Erin were in stitches.

"So how wild will karaoke night get?" said Carrie.

"It's tame and we'll sit in the back, where we always do."

◆◆◆

The next night, the volleyball team, with Carrie in tow, came in for karaoke night. Soon, a group of young women came in and sat near the front. Amber pointed out Sarah. Carrie recognized her. She was pretty, so pretty that you couldn't help but notice when she walked through the union.

Then in walked Brad and several of his friends.

She couldn't help herself. She felt giddy inside when Brad looked in the back and gave her a smile and a wave. She smiled and nodded her head upward, trying to seem casual while she fought the urge to wink at him.

Brad and his friends sat up front. They'd obviously been drinking before they got to the Hofhaus.

Bad boys breaking training.

Brad went up and browsed through the choices, longer than Carrie had expected, for a "regular." Suddenly, he stopped, smiled, and made a selection.

To everyone's surprise, on came the old-fashioned, lush piano sound of "Unforgettable" by Nat King Cole. As the music got to the opening refrain, Brad broke into a surprisingly smooth mimic of a lounge lizard with warped lyrics.

"*Unregrettable,* that's what you are."

Brad proceeded to croon his own altered lyrics, but smooth as a boy band singer with his rendition.

Sarah stared bullets at Brad. His buddies howled in the front, many in the bar were laughing too. In the back, Carrie's table stifled laughs, Carrie giving them a look of "don't you dare."

Brad was finishing a tipsy dance with the stand and mic. Suddenly, Sarah, looking infuriated, got up, said something to her friend, and they both grabbed their jackets and walked out.

As if he were on a romantic date, Brad crooned his final verses and finished with a slow lowering of the microphone stand like a dance partner who was complying with his smooth ballroom finish, while the piano, harp, and sax glided to the end of the iconic song.

Then, as the crowd wildly applauded, laughed, and whistled, Brad gave an expansive, vapid wave to the Haufhaus crowd and yelled, "Thank you, thank you. I'll be here all week!"

The rest of Sarah's friends left quickly, one trying to hide her laughter at her "friend's" expense.

Once they were gone, Carrie and her table broke out laughing and a few whistled as Brad, still taking hammy bows, sat down while several of his friends slapped his back or just shook their heads in disbelief.

Several minutes later, he made his way back to the men's room, crossing an aisle one table in front of the volleyball table.

He stopped when he saw Carrie.

"Why Miss Station, have you enjoyed the singing tonight?"

"I haven't heard any yet," she laughed as she shook her head.

Brad's buddy Ron gently pushed him onward toward the can. Brad was now in full Elvis, "Thank you! Thank you very much!"

Carrie and her friends got up and were out before Brad returned and sang "Bad to the Bone."

Back at her dorm, Carrie went up to study after sticking with cola that night.

She looked out the window above her desk and said quietly, "Brad. He likes me. He mocked a beautiful snot tonight and came back to tease me."

Carrie wasn't used to being thought of as Brad's girlfriend, beautiful, worthy of the BMOC.

Wow, I guess we're not in Kansas anymore, Toto.

11

The Foundation Brunch

"NOT TAKING A back seat for this one? Going for teacher's pet?" Jeff taunted as he slid past Carrie without asking if it was all right to join her. They were in the small auditorium's theatre seating.

"No, Rockhead, I have to leave early for practice in case some of the geology students ask too many questions on apparel," Carrie said looking straight ahead, seeming to enjoy how easily the retort had sprung from her mouth.

Jeff smirked. "So, your team nominated you?"

"Yes, and the computer science dean too," Carrie replied, still looking straight ahead but clearly enjoying the one-ups-man-ship.

"A double nominee! Good, I'm in the right section," said Jeff. "I got one from the dean of the history department. He felt this august body may need some balance and intellect. I guess the ROTC/Guard group thought I cleaned up best too."

Carrie stifled a laugh and smiled. "I thought you didn't want to be one of the long-winded, pseudo-intellectuals from our classes."

Jeff was sharpening a denial when Kathy, Amy's best friend, walked in. She was hurrying to find a seat as the Foundation Director was getting ready to start. Kathy was halfway up the stairs by the left side aisle when she saw Jeff and smiled.

She gave Carrie a startled look when she saw they were in the middle of a joking exchange. "Hey, Jeff," she said as she went past them and walked up several rows more, then inward to the middle of the row. Jeff could feel her look.

Carrie gave him an amused look. "Trouble back at the fort, soldier?" she said in an old, gruff whisper.

Lately there had been some jealous moments by Amy, but he wasn't ready to talk to Carrie about troubles on the home front. Especially not when she seemed to be starting a strong relationship with Brad Kippick.

"Welcome to Foundation Orientation. I'm Mavis, the Foundation Director. I met many of you at your interview already. Congratulations for being chosen. Being a student representative on the Alumni Foundation is an honor and a privilege. You are now part of our public image to our alums."

"Why aren't you saluting, Rockhead?" said Carrie.

I hate it when she does that during a pause. And she's enjoying Kathy looking at me when she talks to me.

Mavis continued. "And with the honor goes responsibility. You are each representing the student body to the alumni and faculty members at the Foundation events. Ten days from now is the Homecoming Saturday reception and brunch with the Foundation. There will be a spring meeting and occasional special events during any given year.

"Now, about appearance and attire. Men, suits or sports coats with conservative ties. Women, dresses that are stylish and not provocative."

Jeff taunted, "Yeah, Carrie, don't wear your Nike's with your prom dress."

As Carrie shot him a bored look, he saw Kathy out of the corner of his eye looking at him and Carrie. It wasn't an angry look, it was more of a curious look.

When the briefing was finished, several students asked additional questions about attire and arrival time.

"You going to come to the Brunch in your uniform and medals, Rockhead?" Carrie asked dryly.

"No, Ms. Station, I'm wearing the classic uniform. Blue blazer, charcoal slacks, and conservative tie. I've got to charm the Blue Hairs."

Carrie smiled. "Good one."

"How about you?" Jeff said. "Going to buff up your Nikes for the brunch?"

"You'll have to wait and see," Carrie said with mock disgust and left before Kathy could come down for a chat.

◆◆◆

THE BRUNCH

"Jeff, wait until you see Amy's dress for the Variety show tonight!" said Kathy as she handed Jeff his name tag.

"She'll look fabulous, dahling," Jeff said in his best Billy Crystal SNL imitation. "Will it go well with my jeans and a corduroy sport coat?"

"Hanford, you're such a smart ass," Kathy laughed quietly. "Sometimes I don't know what she sees in you."

"You don't think I clean up well?" said Jeff as he leaned back for her to look at his pinstripe suit with a Brooks Brothers red tie.

"Your face said different when I walked in," he teased.

"You look fine, Jeffrey," said Kathy as an elderly alumnus asked for her name tag.

Kathy's actually pretty decent. At least she'll be out of here this year and Amy can't bug her about spying anymore.

Jeff walked over to the big doorway to look in at

the reception before wading into the first intimidating event since Sgt. Florence yelled at him last summer at camp.

He froze as he saw her. *Oh God. She's stunning.*

Carrie had walked around the corner at the end of the hallway. She wore a knee-length, muted black dress with a V-neckline that wasn't too plunging. It didn't reveal cleavage, but clung beautifully to her breasts. She had on half pumps, a simple silver necklace, and red lipstick.

Who is this girl? Comes to class in sweats or jeans with loose-fitting sweatshirts. She's elegant and…so beautiful.

Kathy watched while Carrie walked over toward the door.

"Eyes up, Rockhead," said Carrie. "Don't let those Blue Hairs catch you checking them out."

She saw me staring at her breasts…and she's enjoying it!

"Well, better start mixing before the brunch starts," Carrie said.

As they walked, Carrie veered toward two distinguished elderly men standing at a coffee station.

"Be careful, don't make them drool," Jeff said.

"Don't worry. You seem to have that act covered," Carrie shot back with a bemused look as she walked away.

Good girl. Got in the last word. I'm enjoying this Foundation gig.

There were 15 minutes left before the Brunch. Jeff was talking to several alumni when the person everyone knew turned and stuck out his hand.

"Good morning. Garrett Hamilton."

"The Governor" had been a former governor for three years after two terms as one of the state's most popular governors in recent history. They'd been told to call him that for protocol at the briefing.

He shook Jeff's hand firmly.

"Jeff Hanford, sir. From Franklin. It's an honor to meet you. My parents both campaigned for you. My dad took me out with lawn signs and paid me $5 to patrol our precinct with my bike the last 10 days to keep them up."

Ye gods, slow down. What do you want? A scout badge?

The Governor laughed. "That's a great story. Lawn signs after Halloween were always tough."

The Governor paused for a moment and looked more closely at Jeff. "Hanford? Is your dad Charlie Hanford from the Franklin Rotary?"

"Yes, sir."

"How's he doing?" Hamilton asked as he put his hand on Jeff's shoulder.

"He died in a car accident five years ago, sir."

Hamilton's face went somber and he gripped Jeff's shoulder gently. "Jeff, I'm so sorry. I didn't know. How is your mom, the rest of the family?"

"Better, sir. Better. Mom got remarried three

years ago to a widower from our church. We knew him and his family. He's a good guy, sir."

"Jeff, it's Garrett, okay?"

"Yes, Garrett. Got the habit from Guard," said Jeff. "Reflex for sir, then work your way down. Or up, sir!"

"I get you. I get you," laughed Garrett. "National Guard for the Transportation group here?"

"Yes. I'm going pre-law and decided I'd cut down on the college debt two years ago."

"What's your major? What year you in now?"

"History. Geology minor. Junior plus with mid-term graduation December of 2001."

Hamilton turned them away from the crowd. "I want you to take this card. Call my executive assistant next week and ask her about an internship interview, okay?"

The Hamilton Law firm. I can't believe it. Dad said it was the most prestigious one in the state.

"Thank you, I will," said Jeff and shook Hamilton's hand once more. The Governor walked off to circulate some more.

Jeff weaved through the crowd trying to find Carrie. He couldn't wait to tell her what just happened.

As he approached Carrie, she surprised him. She turned and put her arm through his as she pulled him beside her. "Jeff, I'd like to introduce you to Maureen Hamilton, former First Lady and this year's President of the Foundation."

Jeff reached out and shook Maureen's hand.

Carrie's keeping her breast on my arm. Hasn't let go.

"Maureen, Jeff's one of our future leaders."

Jeff was too stunned to say anything as Maureen's eye's twinkled.

God, she's beautiful too.

"If Carrie says you are, I'd better introduce you to Garrett," she laughed.

"No need," Garrett said as he walked up behind Maureen. "I've already got him lined up to apply for next summer's internships. You've got a good man there, Carrie," he said as he looked at Carrie's nametag.

Carrie, with her arm still through Jeff's, blushed as she pulled her arm out and said, "Oh, we're not a couple, just good friends. But he's the one you should be recruiting for your law firm."

Jeff, sensing Carrie's discomfort, looked at Carrie and gave her a smirk.

"I don't know, Governor. I think I've got *too many friends in low places* to be with this woman."

For a second, the remark caused a stunned silence. Then Maureen Hamilton burst out laughing and Garrett joined her.

Carrie pulled back, popped Jeff with a gentle fist to his shoulder and laughed, too.

She gave him a quick look of both appreciation and amusement at his charm.

"Ladies and gentlemen, the brunch buffet is ready," said Mavis. "Take your places at the tables listed on your name tag and please wait until staff tells you to go through the line.

"And first through the line, our President of the Foundation for 2001-2002, Maureen Hamilton."

Carrie and Jeff joined the crowd in applause. They were standing right next to Maureen. Garrett had diplomatically stepped back by Jeff. It was Maureen's day to shine.

People broke off to find their tables. Carrie started to walk toward Table 16.

"I owe you," Jeff said as he gently touched her elbow and leaned toward her while they walked.

"I'll say you do, Rockhead," Carrie whispered back. "I expect study notes ANY TIME I miss a class."

Each student had been assigned a table with foundation patrons and their spouses. Carrie was assigned to Maureen's table. Some patrons were widows, and Mavis, always savvy, had Jeff assigned to the table of a graceful and witty widow of a former Foundation President. Garrett Hamilton was also at Jeff's table.

After they were seated, Jeff saw Garrett glance at Maureen's table, giving her an affectionate look "When Maureen and I first met here, she was one of the first female student body presidents. We met at this brunch our junior year and fell in love. But unlike my political and government dining events, we often divide and conquer at these. And I love the Foundation mission, alumnae contact, and meeting the student leaders like you and Carrie."

After the brunch ended, Garrett found Jeff again. "Maureen and I would like to have you and Carrie join us at the Dean's reception this afternoon around 5:00. It's held before the Homecoming Variety show. We always invite several students from the Foundation.

"Could you two be there? Bring your date if you're on your way to the show, okay?" Garrett turned and left without getting a confirmation. It was like a smiling request from an officer in the military.

"Carrie, you up for a command performance?" asked Jeff as he caught her walking out. He told her about the Governor's "request."

"I'm going to the Variety Show with Brad tonight," she said.

"Good," said Jeff. "Bring him and tell him no karaoke at the President's reception."

Carrie laughed, "That's not likely. He'll be cleaning up and hopefully not hurt from the football game. See you there, Jeff."

12

The Catch

"GET IN, CARRIE. Looking great," said Amber. "We can still park and get up in the stands in time for the kickoff."

They pulled out and sped off for the stadium.

"Thanks for the ride," said Carrie. "This is bizarre. We went to every home football game our freshman year, then last year I didn't go to one. Got wrapped up in volleyball, time with my friends, and studying." She gave Amber an evil grin. "Then two weeks ago, some meddling friend lines up a call from Brad, and here we are."

"Yeah, saved from spinsterhood!" laughed Amber as she turned on the radio to listen to the pre-game while they drove.

"Folks, FSU wants to get back at the Baxter State Redbirds after that 24-3 embarrassment last year," Bernie Hansen, KFSU radio's long-time announcer said in his worried voice. "It's a team game, but a lot may be riding on Adam Grant at quarterback and Brad Kippick, our star wide receiver."

"YEAH, kick ass Brad!" yelled Amber as she fist pumped.

Carrie swatted Amber as they both laughed.

"It's Homecoming and Freeman State's won its first four games," said Bernie. "But this is the first real challenge they've faced so far this year. Stay tuned. You don't want to miss this one. Fifteen minutes to kickoff, folks."

Yeah, go figure, thought Carrie. *I'm going to cheer for Brad, the football star. You don't want to miss this one.*

◆◆◆

It was a beautiful October afternoon for football in the Midwest—62 degrees.

Instead of her usual FSU sweatshirt and jeans, Carrie had on a form-fitting dark sweater and slack outfit that Amber had insisted she get for the homecoming game.

As Amber took the stadium steps two at a time ahead of her up to student seating, Carrie felt the admiring looks from several of the guys on the aisle as she ran up the stairs.

Amber insisted they sit two rows from the top.

With just a few minutes to kickoff, they were seated. Up behind her to the right, Carrie overheard a guy say, "She looks like that volleyball star, but she's hotter."

Suddenly Amber stood up, took off her jacket, and stood there in her bright new FSU sweatshirt. Then she waved.

"Carrie, stand up," she said pulling on Carrie's arm.

There, down on the sidelines behind the bench, was Brad Kippick, #85. He waved up at her while everyone around them suddenly looked at Carrie. She waved back, blushed, and sat down quickly.

One of the guys near them stood up and yelled, "Let's go, Kippick. Beat these guys like a rented mule!" People around them laughed and several gave Carrie a friendly look.

Down on the sideline, Brad smiled, then tossed the football back at Adam for a last throw and high catch before kickoff.

Once the game started, the two teams went at each other in a fierce defensive battle. But Carrie wasn't watching the plays or the game itself. She couldn't take her eyes off Brad. She wanted to see where he ran, who he blocked, what linebacker threw him down when he tried to block him, his catches, and when he was just standing on the sidelines.

"What a sack!" yelled Amber as the defense dropped the Redbirds' quarterback for a 10-yard loss.

"Yeah, okay, great stop," said Carrie.

Amber elbowed her, leaned over and chuckled in Carrie's ear while the FSU students around them went wild. "Carrie, Brad's just standing there on the sidelines. Is he scratching his butt?"

Carrie turned red, didn't look at Amber but elbowed her back. Then, she looked at Amber and they both laughed.

"I can't help it," said Carrie.

"Good!" said Amber. "It's working."

God help me. I'm falling for this charmer...and I'm loving it.

Late in the first half, the Redbirds were ahead 7-0 as FSU drove the ball down to the Redbirds' 20 on runs and short passes. Brad was being lined up both wide right and wide left to keep the defense on their feet. He was the decoy to get others open.

"Why doesn't Adam throw it to Brad?" snapped Carrie.

"Because he can't get open!" Amber said sideways while she kept her eyes on the game. "They've got their all-conference defender on him."

It was third down and eight to go on the 20 with 30 seconds to go to halftime.

"Come on, Brad," Carrie yelled.

"They just need to get the first down," said Amber. "Down and out past the 10-yard line."

Brad lined up wide right. As he ran straight down the field, his defender was on him tight. Brad started right toward the out-of-bounds marker just past the 10-yard line. The defender went with him. Suddenly, Brad stopped on his left foot, did a spin, and was behind the defender. He put up his hand as he ran toward the end zone. Adam had seen him, knew he was going to try the long route, and let the ball fly toward the corner of the end zone.

"Go, go, get it!" yelled Amber.

"GET UNDER IT, BRAD!" screamed Carrie.

Brad ran toward the ball coming down in the back of the right end zone and leaped to catch it. Just as he caught the ball, the safety came over and flew through the air, hitting Brad hard in the back. Brad held on to the ball as he came down. Now he was turned sideways toward the back of the end zone with the defender riding him down with Brad's feet dragging in bounds. The referee had been running back behind the end zone, watched them hit the ground, and stopped to put his hands on both knees as he watched to see if Brad kept hold of it. Then the ref slowly put up both arms for a touchdown.

"HE CAUGHT IT!" shouted Carrie. She hugged Amber as they both laughed and yelled.

Then they looked back. Brad was still down. The defender climbed off him, looked down, and walked away. Slowly, Brad pushed up with his right arm and held the ball up with his left hand.

The stadium erupted. People Carrie didn't know were slapping her and Amber on their backs as if they'd caught it. The guy next to her grabbed her by the shoulders and yelled, "He caught it! Tell him I'll buy him a beer."

"Folks, it's a defensive battle, 7-7," Bernie Hansen said as the halftime break opened on the radio. "They've held Kippick to two catches out of five attempts for 30 yards. But that last one for 20 yards was the catch of the day. Brad Kippick got creamed as he caught it, but he held onto it. We've got an exciting second half coming. Don't go away."

"Well, you can give him a kiss for me tonight," teased Amber as they watched the marching band come on the field. "That was a tough catch. You may have to kiss his owies tonight."

Carrie looked at her with a "not in front of a crowd!" look. Amber just grinned back behind her sunglasses.

"Maybe I will," whispered Carrie in her ear. "He told me last night his roommates had other plans and won't be staying at the apartment tonight."

Amber's face turned serious as she looked back at Carrie over her sunglasses. "All alone at Brad's apartment tonight," she said in her mock Church Lady voice. "How convenient."

Carrie laughed and slugged her shoulder.

The marching band caught Carrie's attention. "What happened to them?" said Carrie as she watched them finish a snappy version of an old marching song. "They're fun. They're good now."

"The old band director retired two years ago," said Amber. "The new one has made them into a great part of the game now."

The band started playing something familiar. "What's that song?" asked Carrie.

"'It's All For You' by Sister Hazel," yelled the guy beside her. The brass was loud and they'd rolled out a trailer with an electric guitarist, bassist, and drum set.

The dance team came out on the field in front of the band. Soon they had the student section on their feet, swinging back and forth in rhythm with the dancers' sexy hip swings.

It was infectious. Down and over on the 50-yard line alum seating, Carrie saw Maureen Hamilton stand up and start swaying like the student section. Soon Garrett and the many of the older alums were up swaying like Maureen. It was intoxicating on a beautiful fall afternoon. By the third chorus, Amber, Carrie, and the student section were singing the words out loud.

After the song ended, Amber leaned over to Carrie and changed the lyrics to it *being all about Brad*. Carrie swatted Amber and winked at her as they reveled in the euphoria of the moment.

The third quarter continued as a defensive game. FSU got stalled on a drive to the 25 but got a field goal to make it 10-7, FSU.

The defensive struggle continued into the fourth

quarter. Brad was only able to catch two more passes. Then with only five minutes left in the game, the Redbirds finished off a long 80-yard drive to score and make it 14-10 with the Redbirds up.

FSU got the ball on the kickoff and drove down the field, got thrown back, and came up stalled near mid-field.

"Well, folks, it's do or die for Freeman State," said Bernie Hansen. "It's time out and FSU is down by four points, 14-10."

Down on the field, FSU's team was huddled up. Adam had been sacked before an attempted screen pass on second and eight could be set up.

Carrie and Amber watched as Coach Farber pointed at Adam, then Brad, then the rest in the huddle. Then he was back to Brad.

"Yikes," said Carrie. "Looks like the coach was chewing Brad out!"

"Wait and see," said Amber. "He may be riding him to be sure to catch it or fake it to be the decoy."

"Adam's running out with Brad separately," said Carrie. "What's with that?

"Okay folks, we're back," said Bernie Hansen. "Everybody is on their feet. The Red Birds have had FSU's number today on third down and long. Let's see how FSU sets up."

Brad got set at wide right. He was 10 yards in from the sideline.

Carrie bit her fingernails. Amber reached over

and pulled her hand down without taking her eyes off the field.

After two short hard counts, Adam got the snap back in shotgun. Brad was already cutting back toward the sideline. Adam did a hard pump fake to Brad, then looked back to the middle. The linebacker stayed ahead of Farrell's crossing pattern. The linebacker slowed and caught Farrell's left ankle as he passed. Farrell went down.

Carrie scanned the football field. *Three guys on Jefferson. Where's Brad? There he is!*

Brad had slowed earlier and his guy had gone to the crossing coverage.

Brad's long gate was doing a deep post behind them now. The safety saw it and sprinted toward Brad.

Adam let fly with his pass just as the Redbirds' big defensive tackle hit him and drove him down hard into the turf.

"Damn, it's too short," Amber yelped.

Brad angled inward. He was on a collision course with the safety if he caught it on the run in the middle of the field. Brad accelerated. At the last second, with the safety ready to hit him head low in the belt, Brad cut back even more to get to the under thrown ball.

"And Kippick is SOARING," yelled Bernie Hansen. "He's caught it flying BACK toward the line. He's weaving. HE STIFF ARMS the linebacker. He's still going! He's starting down the left sideline! The safety is coming back at him! Kippick's at the 30. Safety's got a bead on him. Here it comes. HOLY COW. Kippick just vaulted over the safety as he came in too low. He's headed back toward the middle. The 15, the 10, the 5, AND HE'S IN!"

Carrie and Amber screamed and hugged each other as everyone around them went nuts. Again, strangers behind her were shaking and slapping Carrie's shoulders for Brad's catch.

"LADIES AND GENTLEMEN, KIPPICK JUST SAVED THE DAY!" Bernie Hansen yelled into his microphone. "This crowd is going nuts. Kippick just tossed the ball to the ref and his teammates are swarming all over him. It's pandemonium! That play took 14 seconds but it seemed like forever as Kippick leaped, weaved, and ran his heart out to the other side of the field and then back down the middle to score!"

As he trotted off the field with his teammates mobbing him, Brad looked up in Carrie's direction, smiled, and shook his head like he couldn't believe it either.

"There are still five seconds left," Bernie continued. "The Redbirds are lined up for the on-side kick. Jefferson, Farrell, and Kippick are up front. They've got the 'good hands' players ready to grab this ball."

"Oh, God," Carrie said. "I can't look."

"You'd better," laughed Amber. "You're watching history."

Bernie Hansen called the final seconds. "And here comes the on-side kick. IT'S TAKEN A HIGH SECOND BOUNCE! Kippick is leaping up after it. He's hit! HE FLIPPED OVER THEM! LADIES AND GENTLEMEN, Brad Kippick just got hammered in mid-air and somersaulted over the Redbirds!

"He's on his back, behind them. He's just lying there."

Carrie covered her eyes a second, then put her hands on the side of her cheeks. She held her breath.

"He's raising the ball up. HE HELD ON! FSU WINS!" yelled Bernie. "FSU HAS COME BACK TO UPSET THE REDBIRDS FOR HOMECOMING! Listen to that. This place is going wild. WHAT A DAY FOR FSU!"

As Adam ran out on the field to help him up, Brad looked up in Carrie's section of the stands and shot his grin.

Amber, laughing and clapping, yelled in Carrie's ear, "Well, Brad's never going to have to buy a beer at the Hofhaus for the rest of his life."

Carrie didn't want anyone to see her tearing up, so she yelled. "Way to go, Kippick!"

Amber shoulder hugged Carrie and then gave her some space to breathe it in.

Down on the field, they watched Adam hug Brad. Camera's clicked away furiously on the sidelines.

The picture on the *Sunday Gazette's* banner headline the next day had a two-word caption: *Happy Warriors.*

13

The President's Reception

"WELL, LOOKS LIKE your date's getting a manicure or something. A no-show," teased Jeff.

"Yeah, gotta' let the big dog bark," laughed Carrie. "Something tells me he's at his apartment having a brew before going to the Hofhaus to join in the fun. You know, he really doesn't have a big head. Who knew?"

"I know, I know," Jeff laughed. "Hell, I'd be his date tonight."

"Yeah, well he's taken, Rockhead. Better stick with Amy. Is she a no-show too?"

"Yup. She's planned this after-the-game fashion and hair prep event for weeks. Begged off. Guess we're stuck with each other." He smiled his disarming grin.

Yeah, go figure. The former spinster talking to the Governor's new protégé and going to the Variety Show with the star of the game.

"Speaking of fashion," said Carrie, "You stepped up and wore your pin stripes this afternoon. Funeral later?"

"You're just full of yourself now, aren't you?" said Jeff as he laughed.

She caught him staring at her and sensed it was time to switch gears. "This place isn't as forbidding as it looked when I was a scared freshman two years ago."

"Same here," said Jeff.

A few minutes later, Garrett Hamilton broke away from chatting with the president of the university, Dean Winters, and came over to say hello to Carrie and Jeff.

Garrett turned to Carrie. "Maureen tells me you're a double major in computer science and history. Right?"

"Not quite, Governor. Information technology major with a history minor."

"That's my problem," Garrett said. "I don't even know what they call it as a major now. I majored in business, but I can't figure out how to do spreadsheets on our computer at home, and I don't have the technical support like I did as Governor."

Maureen joined them and nodded in bemusement

at Garrett's admission. "Now this rise of the internet, searches, and websites. I'm lost and I don't want to have to call my old frat brother here at the computer department again. He lorded it over me that I had to ask him for help on documents, spreadsheets, and logging in.

"I've been asked to join a new commission on better integration of state and federal emergency response for disasters, floods, and civil defense. It's important, but it will involve the internet. I don't want to be embarrassed."

Before Carrie could speak, Jeff leaned in. "Governor, Carrie's the best at explaining computers, networks, and the internet to tech stooges like me. She's better than most teachers at dumbing it down. She's not just another pretty face."

Carrie almost laughed at how red Jeff's face got.

"I didn't…I mean…" Jeff stammered. He shook his head. "That came out all wrong."

Garrett just laughed and looked from Jeff to Carrie. "Carrie, could I get some advice occasionally from you by phone or maybe email? I'm in way over my head. I get some occasional commissions or board meeting minutes by email that I can't even open!"

"Governor, I'd be honored to help you. It is kind of daunting to keep up with some of this right now. I can give you my cell phone and my Hotmail address if we can find a note pad."

"Hotmail? That sounds kind of racy," Garrett chuckled as Maureen shook her head.

"Our friends use that and he doesn't even notice it," Maureen laughed.

Garrett reached in his lapel and pulled out a beige business card with the bright gold lettering of his law firm and *Governor Garrett Hamilton* at the top. Carrie held it for several seconds, suddenly in awe that she was holding the former Governor's business card and being asked for help. When he handed her his gold pen, she turned it over and wrote her cell phone and email address on it.

Garrett looked at it and handed it to Jeff. "Can I have your phone and address…email, too?"

Jeff wrote both down below Carrie's and handed it back to him. Then, in a graceful, fluid motion, Garrett Hamilton handed each of them a fresh card and said, "Thanks, Carrie. Thanks, Jeff. In these crazy times, the impeachment, the press, and now this campaign, it's great to see the two of you as part of our future. If you need to, please call Maureen or I. We both think a lot of you two and we don't give out this home number often."

Maureen smiled with a firm nod, then she and Garrett broke away to return to the President and his wife.

Carrie and Jeff watched them walk away, then looked down at their gold-lettered business cards.

"Well, Computer Czaress, you're not going to rat

me out to the Governor if I break any protocol, are you?"

"No, I'd never do that," Carrie replied as she looked up. It was more intimate than she'd meant but she was overwhelmed by what had just happened.

"I know, Carrie," Jeff replied. "You were classy when you assured him the internet is overwhelming and you'd keep him from being a tech idiot."

"No thanks to you, Rockhead! Making me out to be the world's computer expert and setting me up to be his unpaid, on-call computer geek," Carrie said with mock anger and a smile she couldn't control.

"Damn, it's 7:00, Carrie," Jeff said as he looked at the clock on the wall. "We've got to get going."

They walked out the foyer and into the cool October night.

"Well, guess I'll have to find a safe place for this card in case I ever need a favor from the Governor," Jeff said as he put it in his lapel pocket.

"Yeah, I'll have to keep mine safe, too." Carrie slowly put it inside her dark bra under the black V-necked dress she'd worn. She knew Jeff was looking sideways, watching her as they walked down the steps of the President's front walk.

Jeff missed the last step and tripped into a sideways stumble before recovering as his feet hit the sidewalk.

"I meant to do that," Jeff said in his best Pee Wee Herman voice.

Carrie laughed so hard she snorted at Jeff's disarming way of waltzing out of another embarrassing moment.

"Well, Rockhead, hope your card is safe," she laughed. She turned left and gave a quick wave over her shoulder as she looked back.

Jeff stood for a moment and watched her walk away. *God, Brad doesn't know how lucky he is. Carrie was glowing tonight. She was just beautiful,* he thought as he turned and walked the opposite way. *And Amy would kill me if she knew what I was thinking. And she'll kill me if we're late.*

◆◆◆

THE VARIETY SHOW

The Variety Show was in decline but still something Jeff needed to attend since he was on the Foundation and Amy was on Panhellenic Council.

"Whew, we made it," said Jeff as he and Amy came in at 7:25, sitting down on the left side of the Auditorium.

Amy's blonde hair was swept back in a tight bun that accented her low cut, slender blue dress that hugged her petite figure.

"Amy, you look incredible," Jeff said as he looked at her after they'd been seated.

"Well, about time you noticed," she said as she looked back at him.

Jeff felt a twinge of guilt. Amy had been sweet to him when he was unsure of himself two years ago when they first dated. Tonight, she looked like an unattainable dream for Jeff, the clumsy freshman of three years ago.

"I'm noticing, I'm noticing," he said as he leaned over and gave her a gentle kiss on the cheek.

Brad and Carrie came in just after them. They sat over on the right side, a couple of rows ahead. Brad was "the star" that night, but didn't overplay it. He acknowledged some catcalls and applause from seats near them with a "cool it" gesture.

Carrie caught Jeff's eye across the rows and nodded. Others around Jeff and Amy were saying how great Brad's catch and run had been.

"How was the reception at the President's?" asked Amy.

"It was great. I've been invited by the Governor to apply for an internship at the Hamilton Law Firm next summer."

"Well, I wouldn't mind being married to a good looking, smart lawyer someday," Amy said as she winked at him.

God help you, Amy. You really crave status.

He thought better of telling her the rest of the afternoon's news. How he and Carrie were invited as THE two Foundation students by Garrett and

Maureen Hamilton to the President's reception. That they had been asked to write their names down on the Governor's business card together. *Like a couple.*

Carrie was still brimming with the exciting news that the Governor had asked her to be his on-call computer expert. As flattered and excited as she was, she didn't share the news with Brad.

How could she tell him that she and Jeff were considered special by Garrett and Maureen Hamilton? It just didn't sound quite right. Carrie looked at Brad and her mind drifted off of Jeff. Here she was, sitting with Brad, "The Star." A ton of women at the variety show would love to be her.

Life was good. It was great to have good friends like Jeff. A separate guy, separate world, with no strings attached.

Tonight, she was Brad Kippick's new girlfriend. He was tall, lanky, super athletic, good looking, funny, sexy…and her guy.

Eat your hearts out, girls.

14

Hatchet

FRIDAY, SEPTEMBER 8, 2000

"SO YOU'RE VOTING for Gore?" asked Jeff.

"Yeah, wish it was Bradley," said Carrie. "So you're voting for Bush?"

"Yeah, wish it was McCain. So does Dave. I don't see a strong Commander in Chief in either one of them after their campaigns," Jeff said with disgust. "But they both have more respect for the military than the one I serve under now."

Carrie nodded. *No argument on that one, Rockhead.*

"The country is so angry and partisan after the impeachment, what's fair game, who had affairs..." Jeff paused.

"And who gets to stay in office after affairs," said Carrie.

She smiled as they rounded the stairs to get down to first floor.

"Find that funny, Station?" Jeff asked, with a little edge in his voice.

Carrie looked at Jeff apologetically, eyes widened, "Oh, no," she said. "No. I was laughing at our attitudes. We aren't candidate or party worshipers. More like skeptical realists."

They were at the bottom of the stairs outside Fleener Hall, ready to go their separate ways.

Jeff looked at her and smirked, "Yeah, skeptical realists."

Then as she started up the sidewalk to the library, Jeff looked over his shoulder and gave her the grin. "Yeah, but mine's gonna win."

Carrie looked back, rolled her eyes, and turned back toward the library.

Rockhead, you can go from nearly decent to smartass in a nanosecond. You charming bastard.

◆◆◆

SATURDAY, SEPTEMBER 9, 2000

That September, Freeman State's women's volleyball team started growing a "reputation." When the coach allowed an open practice for fans after the first home football game, the team and their warm-up music rotation became a sensation.

"Good Vibrations" by Marky Mark Funky Bunch was followed up by "Tubthumping" by

Chumbawamba, then "What is Love?" by Haddaway, and they finished with "Vogue" by Madonna.

"Man, they're hot!" Dave had said when Amy and Nicole were out of earshot.

"I know," whispered Jeff.

"Especially Carrie, huh?" whispered Dave.

Jeff shot him a STFU look.

❖❖❖

MONDAY, OCTOBER 2, 2000

"Jeff, let's go to the women's first volleyball game Thursday," said Dave on his cell.

"Look, Dave, I *will* make it to drill this weekend."

"Shit. You're with Amy. Can't talk?" said Dave.

"YES. Yes. I'll bring the poncho I borrowed," said Jeff. "You're worse than Sgt. Florence. Lighten up. I'll see you in class."

"That Dave," said Amy. "He's a persistent little jerk at times."

You have no idea.

❖❖❖

"See, I told you we could do this. No sweat," said Dave.

"Yeah, well, telling Amy I was going to study and then take a break with you later is going to sound lame if she hears I was here with you," said Jeff.

"You only have to wear dog tags once a month,"

said Dave as they walked in the large gym. "She might as well have a dog's shock collar on you, Hanford. You are so P.W."

"Yeah? Well at least I have a girlfriend."

Dave ignored Jeff's comment and looked up at the bleachers. "Carrie told me to make sure we get a good seat before they come out for warm-ups at 6:30."

"Why?" whispered Jeff.

"Because she winked when she said it!" laughed Dave as he pulled Jeff's jacket sleeve.

They got seated at 6:27 p.m.

At 6:30, the women's volleyball team, led by Melissa and Carrie, the co-captains, ran out through a curtain opening near the gym door. The 25-30 fans in the bleachers applauded and cheered.

Just as Melissa threw up the ball for her first practice serve, on came Shania Twain's "Man, I Feel like a Woman." As the ball hit just inside the back line, Shania was off and running. The song did its magic with the team and the audience. The team looked different in their new, shiny uniforms, and the infectious music and lyrics had the audience clapping and stomping.

"See, I told you we should come early," yelled Dave.

"Yeah, I see why," said Jeff as he watched Carrie jump high to take a set and spike it down the right line.

Man, she looks like she feels like a woman.

The team went through the rest of the warm up with "Girls Just Want to Have Fun" by Cindy Lauper and "Lady Marmalade" by Christina Aguilera, Lil' Kim, Mya, and Pink.

In two weeks, they had doubled the attendance. By the end of the season, their bleachers were full, and the Hofhaus was nearly empty until their game was over. The gym's rafters rocked with fans singing and clapping along with the music during warm ups. They were good and now guys were coming to see…*the women* play volleyball.

◆◆◆

TUESDAY, NOVEMBER 7, 2000

"TUBTHUMPING" BY CHUMBAWAMBA was blaring from the gym's stereo system. Today was the last full practice before Thursday's big game against Wolf State.

Erin taunted Carrie as she gave her a set. "WOLF STATE. OWWWhhhhoooooo."

Carrie sailed forward and spiked one inside the back line. "They couldn't have been named better," Carrie said. "Their players even look angry, on the prowl for an attack."

After last year's crushing loss, it wasn't hard to get ready for Wolf State, their archrival. They were going to be ready this year.

◆◆◆

FSU VS WOLF STATE
THURSDAY, NOVEMBER 9, 2000

"We're rolling. We can do this!" yelled Melissa in the huddle. It was game point for FSU with Wolf State serving.

"This team's come back all year," yelled Carrie above the noise. "Let's show ourselves and this crowd it's been worth it. READY?!"

"F S U Fight!"

In the stands, Jeff was standing with everyone else. He and Dave had come to every home game since October, with or without their girlfriends. Tonight, Amy was along.

Carrie looked at the score board.

Okay, we need to finish off Wolf State with a killer.

Carrie walked back out on the court talking with Melissa, then Erin. By luck, she was where she wanted to be. On the front line, where she could spike. Just as she had settled into her stance, a yell came from above the cheering crowd.

"Come on, Carrie. GIVE 'EM THE HATCHET!"

It was Jeff Hanford. No mistaking that voice. Carrie looked straight ahead at the Wolf State team, trying to stay focused.

I'm gonna kill him.

Mason, Wolf State's best server, threw the ball

above and ahead of her with a beautifully timed serve. It looked like a sure ace through the seam on FSU's side of the court. Sammie dove to her left and got a dig with her left hand nearly pancaked. The ball went sideways to the left. Erin ran under it, 10 feet out of bounds. With her back to Carrie and the front line, she blindly sent a high, arcing set up that came down toward the far right side of their net.

Carrie had dropped back when Erin went out of bounds. She took several steps forward, then launched into an 18" vertical leap as she sailed toward the net with the ball coming down. Her body arced with knees bent, feet back, and her top torso bent back as her right arm came from behind her shoulder. The ball was still three feet back and above the net as Carrie delivered a thundering spike. It shot downward between two blockers, ricocheted off the back defender's leg, and sailed out of bounds.

The FSU crowd erupted. Carrie came back from the net. As Erin ran toward her, she stretched her arm out. Erin pointed back to Sammie.

The ritual started. Carrie's fingers were clasped with Erin's, Erin's with Sammie's, and the rest of the team came together as their clasped hands formed FSU's trademark post-game celebration huddle.

Then, all of the clasped hands rose toward the ceiling. Carrie's hand let loose of the others, symbolically pointing her index finger upward. The rest of the team joined in, pointing toward the rafters, too.

"HATCHET! HATCHET! HATCHET!" Carrie looked up in the stands. He looked like a freshman, down front in the bleachers. Then two of his friends joined in. "HATCHET! HATCHET! HATCHET!" It started to ripple across the crowd. Soon most of the FSU stands were yelling, "HATCHET! HATCHET! HATCHET!"

After the team had broken the huddle to hug each other, Carrie looked up at the stands.

Rockhead, where are you? I'm going to kill you.

Carrie turned and ran back, yelling to the team. Soon they were back in a huddle, all holding hands in a circle. Then a chant rose from their huddle.

"FSU, FSU, FSU."

Carrie pulled out of the huddle, still holding Erin's hand. Each teammate behind her was still holding another teammate's hand. Carrie slowly led them in curl, then into a straight line in front of the bleachers. The team was still chanting "FSU, FSU, FSU."

The crowd joined them. "FSU, FSU, FSU. FSU, FSU, FSU."

Then, on Carrie's lead, the FSU women's volleyball team raised its arms above them. Carrie and the team screamed, "FSU, FSU, FSU," along with the crowd.

She looked up in the bleachers. There was Jeff. Chanting, "FSU, FSU, FSU." Next to him was a less-than-excited-looking Amy.

I'll still kill you, Rockhead.

◆ ◆ ◆

The next morning, Erin's freshman brother, Freddie was up early, selling newly screen-printed gray T-shirts for $20 outside the Union. Sales were going well.

The T-shirt had four words, two across the top, two across the bottom: "Give 'em The Hatchet." In the middle of the front was a vintage Carry Nation hatchet.

They continued to sell well until Erin got a call from Carrie. Carrie then called Freddie with his choices at his sales headquarters on the Union steps. Within an hour, Freddie had seen the light.

He had chosen life over T-shirt sales.

He surrendered the screen print, artwork and remaining T-shirts to Erin. He got to keep the $400 in revenues he'd made. Luckily for him, it covered all of his expenses with $50 left over.

With all rights to the T-shirts and the artwork, the team got all future sales revenue from the remaining T-shirts. They put them into a split fundraiser for a women's shelter and team uniforms.

At 12:58 that afternoon, Carrie walked briskly into Professor Thompson's *History of the Renaissance and Reformation* and eyed Jeff in his usual seat. On the way down her aisle, she saw it.

He was wearing one of the Hatchet T-shirts and grinning.

"Jeff Hanford, you ASSHOLE!" barked Carrie. She stopped and stood over him. She gripped his T-shirt by the neck and leaned over, in his face.

"I ought to strangle you with this," she said. "I'm the laughing stock of the campus after your showboat yell last night. One of the greatest nights we'll ever know as a team. If I EVER see you wearing this on campus again, *I'll kill you.*"

Jeff's face was part terror, part resignation.

"That's about what I heard on the walk back from the game last night," said Jeff as she dropped him back in his seat. "I guess I'm really on a roll."

"Ahem." It was Professor Thompson. "If the War of the Roses is nearly over back there, let's cover the St. Bartholomew's Day Massacre this afternoon."

I'm going to KILL him.

15

Family Legacy

SPRING 2001

"I'M GOING TO teach the Revolutionary War differently in high school than the way I was taught in high school," Dave said to Carrie as they walked up the steps to Fleener Hall. "I heard that Thompson teaches it differently, too.

"My advisor told us that Thompson teaches *The American Revolution and its War* with the politics, international relations, factions, and even some military battle maps of the war."

"Is he going to have Rockhead come running in with the flag at the end like Mel Gibson in *The Patriot*?" asked Carrie.

"I might if I think it'll help the Yanks," said Jeff from behind them.

"Carrie, Mel Gibson plays your type of guy," Jeff

deadpanned. "Chops up Frogs and Limeys with a hatchet in two straight wars."

"God help us," said Carrie. "I thought we'd get to have a class without you."

Carrie feigned disgust. She knew Jeff would be in the class.

"Sorry," said Dave. "Rockhead and I've been planning on taking this together for over a year."

Oh, I can't resist, thought Carrie.

"You guys sound like Chandler and Joey in their recliners," said Carrie toward Jeff. "Did you run out of videos of *Independence Day* and *Armageddon* at Plainfield on Guard weekend?"

Jeff gave Dave an irritated look, then turned back toward Carrie.

"No, Ms. Station," said Jeff, "We both realized that we wanted to get a class where the American Revolution's factions and military battles were dealt with more vividly. Can you grasp that five-dollar concept or want it in the one-dollar version?"

"That sounded like the ten-cent edition, Rockhead," whispered Carrie as Thompson began taking roll for the new semester.

◆◆◆

Jeff watched Carrie wait at the end of the aisle after the next class for the trio together, *Military History from Napoleon to the Present*.

"What did you mean about teaching the Revolutionary War 'more vividly'?" she asked Dave.

Dave waited for a few of their classmates to file past.

"I meant we were freezing our asses off in our tent after a sleet storm at Ft. Lee, Virginia a year ago," whispered Dave.

Carrie laughed, then caught Jeff's eye. He'd moved to sit on top of the desk behind her. He was glad when she sat down between him and Dave.

"Okay, grunts," she smirked. "School me on your Valley Forge days. I can wait an hour to go to the gym."

"It was AIT for Transportation," said Dave. "Jeff and I were wet and chilled to the bone, out in a two-man pup tent on the last week of field training. We'd gotten drenched with a cold rain that turned to sleet when we stopped for the night. We had to set up a perimeter, pitch our tent, and eat …with our Humvee stuck in the mud next to us, but we could *not* sleep in it during training."

"So, we're wet, cold, and miserable," said Jeff. "We had MRE's…Meals Ready to Eat that had heat chemicals for our meals."

"Yeah," said Dave. "I'm hugging my Chicken Cavatelli pack as it heats up to get *me* warm."

"You guys had hot dating lives then, didn't you," laughed Carrie. "How did you fit Rockhead into a pup tent?"

Jeff shook his head at her. He tried not to let her see how much he was looking at her as she looked back and forth.

Her eyes are so beautiful and fun. I've got to stay focused.

"It's funny now, but it wasn't then," said Dave. "That's when Jeff, teeth chattering in a sleeping bag, started talking about the Revolutionary War. How it had been such a 'near thing.' How we nearly lost so many times and how our wins were so tenuous. Taking Trenton after Christmas in 1776 may have saved the Revolution."

"It's true," said Jeff. "It's an insult today to hear pundits and nimrods on a media panel joke about Washington crossing the Delaware. They are so cliché and ignorant about how it feels to stay out in bad weather and carry on. They think waiting for a cab or latte for five minutes is real suffering.

"Most people don't understand how demoralized the men were in that iconic picture. Some were literally counting the last *six days* until their one-year enlistment ended." Jeff gestured with his hand. "In more sleet and raging wind than that picture shows. The size of the ice chunks was probably exaggerated in the picture, but the rest was worse."

Carrie looked thoughtful. "I'd never thought about it like that…about how awful it must have been for them. Worse than Plainfield."

Jeff rolled his eyes but continued.

"When those miserable guys got out of their boats in the early morning hours, Washington urged them on with leadership we don't see in today's lot.

Except for Colin Powell. He's Army," Jeff said with a grin.

Carrie nodded. "So they went right up the banks into Trenton?"

"No. They first did a forced march on a frozen road for seven or eight miles," said Jeff. "And a lot of them wore rags on their feet. A few were *barefoot."*

Carrie raised her eyebrows in sober surprise.

"The last incredible feat was the attack at daylight, some with just bayonets because their powder was wet," said Dave. "Washington got those men to attack a well-fed force in warm barracks. He guessed right. They surprised the sentries and were able to take 800 hungover Hessians. We had injuries during the battle, but the two who died were from exposure the night before from marching barefoot. They had left a trail of red blood in the snow."

"THAT'S vivid," Jeff said.

Carrie looked from Jeff back to Dave, obviously moved.

"You're right," she said. "We don't teach American History in high school like we should."

Dave glanced at the clock at the front of the classroom. "Whoa, gotta run," Dave said, already on his feet. "Forgot a date," he said over his shoulder.

Carrie got up with Jeff.

"He can refight the Revolution, but can't keep a date," chuckled Jeff.

"You guys finish each other's sentences like a cadence," said Carrie. "It's like you grew up as brothers."

"He is like my brother," said Jeff. "I'd go into battle with him."

Jeff glanced at Carrie. Something about the quiet way she walked beside him made him want to talk more.

"My dad talked that way about Ray," Jeff continued. "They were on the same mortar squad covering one area of their firebase in Vietnam.

"One night a company of VC attacked their side of the firebase. They were off-shift but came out of the dugout in their helmets and boxers. Dad was ahead of Ray as they ran to help cover the guys already firing the mortars. Some VC were already coming over the embankment into the firebase. One had jumped over and was turning to fire at Dad. Ray shot him on the run but the guy slashed him in the side with his bayonet as Ray ran by toward Dad.

"Dad heard it, turned around, and shot two more on the run while he got back to Ray. The VC beside Ray was dead. Ray had a bad stab wound in his right side. Dad took out his .45 and fired at the VC as they came toward the embankment while Ray pulled out his wound bandage. Dad slung both their M-16s over his shoulder and covered Ray while he pulled his .45 out. Dad had Ray take off ahead of him along the embankment. Ray fired left-handed while holding his wound with his right. Dad fired cover behind on the run. He dropped his .45 when the clip emptied and swung one of the M-16s off his shoulder and fired left-handed as he ran behind Ray," chuckled Jeff.

"What's funny about that?" asked Carrie.

"They were both right handed," laughed Jeff. "They couldn't fire for shit with their left.

"Anyway, they got to the mortar guys and dropped down to one on each side of them. They both fired, with their right hands, for nearly 15 minutes of incoming mortar and VC. Dad got a shoulder wound from a VC who came over the embankment firing.

"When the battle stopped, they didn't know how many VC might be inside the firebase. They stayed put for three more hours until sunrise. They could see about 15 dead or dying VC inside with medics crouching over our guys as they made their way to Dad, Ray, and the others."

"I can see why some of the men who've been in war bond together," said Carrie quietly. "Did your Dad and Ray stay in touch later?"

"In 1990, they got to see each other one last time at a firebase reunion in Chicago. They joked that they had "Purple Heart" wounds, but no tickets home. They got put in for Bronze Stars, but it got snafued up the chain of command. But they had each other's backs.

"Ray died in '93. I think it was a drunk driving

accident, but I never asked Dad after he got back from the funeral in Kentucky. It was like Dad had lost one of his brothers. They didn't see each other for 20 years, but they could finish each other's sentences."

They had stopped and sat on the far side of the building on a bench where there was little traffic. The late afternoon sun crept down the wall across from them.

Jeff noticed Carrie's brow furrow as she started to talk again.

"Your dad and Ray had so much courage," Carrie said quietly.

Jeff smiled. "You know what Dad said? '*What choice did we have?*' And he laughed about it," chuckled Jeff. "There was a lot of Grandpa Tom in him."

"Is Grandpa Tom still alive?" asked Carrie.

"Yeah. He's going to be 80 next year. Grandma Jean's gone," Jeff said, gazing at the sun's reflections. "Now he claims he's *really* leader of the clan."

Carrie laughed with Jeff.

"He has an incredible story for his war, too. World War II," said Jeff. "He flunked the physical and wouldn't have had to go. He'd ruptured his left testicle in what we'd call a sports injury today. He was drafted for the Navy around '43. He went for his physical with two hometown guys. Both of them were passed. He was embarrassed and wanted to serve, but the doctor told him no service would take him for the lifting problems from the wound. He asked if there was any way he could get in.

"The doctor said, 'Yes, have the operation.'

"So, as Grandpa Tom likes to say, 'on his own time and own dime,' he had the operation. He gave his left nut to serve in World War II," Jeff said in a matter-of-fact voice.

Carrie raised her head and gave Jeff a look of mild shock. He met her gaze, then looked back at the setting sun reflection on the wall.

"He served on the *USS Bunker Hill*, a carrier, in the Pacific. It's famous for taking two hits from kamikazes with bombs. Nearly 400 killed, over 200 more injured. Grandpa had burns, but helped fight the fires and evacuate guys who were badly injured. He doesn't like to talk about it, but often says the Battle of Okinawa was the biggest for losses, but seems to be the forgotten battle of WW II.

"You're really proud of those guys, aren't you?" said Carrie.

Jeff was touched by the unexpected tenderness in her voice. "Yeah. And once again, it's you who gets me to spill my guts." Jeff grinned as he shook his head at her.

"Have you ever told your sister those stories like you just told them to me?" asked Carrie as she gently put her hand on his arm.

Her touch felt warm, comforting. "No, Dad said she shouldn't hear those when she's so young."

"She's a young woman in college now, like me," said Carrie. "She deserves to hear what I just got to hear. *Soon.* Okay?"

With that, Carrie got up and said, "I hate to go, but I promised Brad I'd meet him. See you tomorrow."

He watched her leave, wishing she could stay with him instead of meeting Brad. Jeff couldn't stop thinking about her eyes—their emotion, their intensity, and how beautiful they were. It was those eyes and the kind way she listened to him that made him open up. Amy would never have listened to war stories like that. She would shut him down before he even got started.

❖❖❖

On Memorial Day weekend, 2001, Jeff took his sister, Suzy, as his "date" to the opening night of *Pearl Harbor.*

Afterwards, they brought ice cream home and took bowls of it out on the back porch swing, like they had as kids.

He told her Dad's Vietnam stories and Grandpa Tom's World War II stories. Suzy cried as she leaned on Jeff's shoulder, for the first time in years. Jeff cried with her. They had a family legacy and now she knew it too. Thanks to Carrie.

16

Out of the Woods

SPRING 2001

"WOW, FORGET STUDYING for now," said Jeff. "I'm going to text Dave and see if he wants to do the stadium/woods run this afternoon."

"Spring fever, Rockhead?" said Carrie as they walked out of Fleener Hall at 3:00 p.m.

"Yeah, I can't study with this beautiful weather," said Jeff. "You still going to go study at the library with this?" Jeff mockingly swung his hand at the bright sun above the Campanile.

"Yup, got to study," said Carrie "Two tests Friday."

"Okay. See you Friday," he said, not looking back as he walked off.

Amy's home for her mom's emergency appendectomy until Friday. I'm a free man.

It was Wednesday. One of those warm, humid afternoons in April that are intoxicating on a Midwest campus after a long winter. Some of the women were sunbathing by Lang Hall, listening to Destiny's Child. Jeff pretended not to look their way as he walked toward the stadium. Several guys were throwing a Frisbee near them, as if that was their only reason to be there. Some lulled to sleep as they basked in the sun.

It had turned hotter and sticky humid by the time Jeff and Dave started their run out past the stadium going west on the path into the woods. It would go back to the edge of the woods bordering the open field, turn north, then curl back around for the mile back to the stadium.

"Man, those look mean," said Dave, pointing at some black clouds on the horizon as they got to the back of the woods. It was 4:30 p.m.

Carrie pulled her earphones and portable CD player from her backpack in the library. Dave Matthews Band, loud for a 10-minute break at a cubicle back in the corner. She relaxed for another song. She soon fell asleep with her head on the desk, no longer visible from the stairway on the second floor.

At 5:00 p.m., large dark clouds developed in the west, covering the sun. Sunbathers and Frisbees were gone. It suddenly got cooler and too calm. Jeff and Dave kicked their speed up for the last 200 yards to get to the big trees next to the stadium parking lot.

"Well, that's enough before the rain comes," said Dave. "Want a ride back?"

"No, I'm going to run a race with the rain back to my apartment. I'll get across campus in time."

As Jeff ran back toward campus on the sidewalk beside the stadium, he realized it was getting much too dark. He looked behind to see ominous, black clouds rolling in.

The emergency warning siren blared, on its mid-campus pole by the library. The black wall of clouds was coming over the trees. In a bizarre moment, Jeff thought they looked like the alien space ship hovering in *Independence Day.* The wind whipped the tree limbs back and forth, making some of them crack and break.

Jeff's adrenaline kicked in, sending him into a full sprint straight toward campus. Half a mile away, he saw some students running in all directions to get out of the library, to get to safety.

His heart leapt into his throat. Carrie was in the library. He told himself she was okay, that she was already safe in the basement.

He looked back again and saw it. The funnel cloud was sweeping through the woods on a northeasterly track, then it cut east. Young buds, limbs, and whole tree trunks were sucked into the roaring wind of the vortex as it broke out of the woods.

Carrie had slept through the tornado warning on the overhead speakers. Her earphones kept her from hearing anything over her CD until she heard the distinct emergency siren right outside. She awoke with a jolt, and stashed her books and player in her backpack. She looked around as she ran down the hall toward the stairs. The library was deserted. *I'm the last out!* She took the stairs two at a time on the way down to first floor. She was headed for Fleener Hall with its marked tornado shelter in its giant basement.

As the funnel cloud broke out of the woods, it crossed the back driveway. It hit the press box on the top of the stadium. An explosion of wood, drywall, and glass erupted out of the press box as the funnel split a 10-foot wide swath through it like a buzz saw. Jeff glanced over his shoulder to see it swerve a little onto a northeasterly path again toward Lang Hall and the other dorms on that side of campus.

Jeff swerved off on a southeast path across the grass toward Fleener Hall. He ran around the back of the library, trying to put the library between him and the tornado. Behind him, the tornado cut back to a straight path up the middle of campus, straight east toward the Campanile.

As Jeff made his turn to run beside the library, he heard and felt the suction from the funnel cloud. As the tornado approached, its suction pulled the Campanile's large bells out against its frame. They clanged as they swung back, only to be violently pulled back again.

The twister veered just in front of the Campanile, but the bottom of the funnel hit the base of its foundation. Chips and whole bricks were blown off by the power of the tornado.

It sounded like a war. The gonging bells were replaced by what sounded like the staccato of machine guns of different timbres as the wood, plywood slabs, and glass from the press box peppered the bell tower.

Jeff had just flanked the front side of the library when he saw her run out.

"Carrie!" He swerved toward her, pointed right, and yelled, "Fleener!" Fleener Hall was 30 yards ahead of them.

"JEFF, DUCK!" Carrie yelled as she swung her hand down. Jeff ducked down and did a shoulder somersault on the ground, stopped and looked up as a steel gardening post flew end over end just above where he would have been.

Jeff got back up and joined Carrie on the run toward Fleener.

They had to get up those 10 stair steps, in the door, and down to the basement.

As they took two to three steps at a time up the stairs, they were pelted with wood, glass, tree debris, and dirt as the funnel caught up with them. A tree limb the size of a baseball bat swirled past Jeff and hit Carrie as she was headed up the stairs. It clipped her right shoulder before it hit her neck and ear. It knocked her over against the rail and brick stair wall.

Jeff slid to a stop on the steps. Carrie was stunned, her head leaning against the bricks. Jeff grabbed her under the arms, pulled her up the stairs, pulled open the door against the deafening wind, and held it with his back as Carrie regained her balance. Once they were inside, Jeff held her arm around his neck and they stumbled down the stairs to the basement together.

The glass doors above them exploded inward from the tornado's wind, glass, and debris. Jeff and Carrie were both pelted in the back and on the head as they reached the bottom of the stairs.

Jeff pulled Carrie sideways the last few feet to the left at the bottom of the stairwell. As she sat down, he swung her backpack off and put it behind their heads, leaning together. It served as a clumsy shield as they continued to get pelted with debris for another 20-30 seconds.

As it subsided, Jeff dropped the backpack beside him on the floor. He looked down at Carrie. His breathing was hard, Carrie's was light. He gently put his hand under her chin and pulled her up from her slump to look at him. She had a gash behind her ear and was bleeding where the limb had clipped her. The blood from the cut had already started soaking the collar of her light polo shirt.

"Do you have tissues or a cloth in your backpack?" yelled Jeff over the wind shrieking down the stairs.

"Yeah, there are some in there," said Carrie as she tried to pull herself up to get her backpack. "OHHH!" she groaned. She slumped back down, leaning into his shoulder, and closed her eyes.

"I'll get some out, okay?" said Jeff. He zipped it open—found books, a laptop, and T-shirt. He went to the side pockets. Pens, lipstick, and small scissors. Her eyes were still closed.

Oh God, I've got to get her something to stop this bleeding.

"Lean against the door," Jeff said. "I'm going to the bathroom to get some paper towels, okay?"

Carrie mumbled, nodded.

Jeff popped open the door, saw the machine on the wall, and ran in. He washed his hands first and caught his reflection in the mirror. He had pockmarks of blood and dirt on his face from where they had been pelted.

It was raining, but the wind had died down as Jeff got back with wet and dry paper towels. He tucked the feminine napkin inside a paper towel, then started to clean her cut. She yelped again.

"I know it hurts, but we've got to clean your cut, compress it, and get your neck wrapped," Jeff said.

"Okay, Hawkeye," mumbled Carrie. "Just don't expect me to swoon like the nurse at summer camp."

"Don't worry," said Jeff. "It's easier with the blow-up dolls in field class."

Carrie laughed and coughed. She looked up. "Damn you, Rockhead," Carrie whispered. "You get me vulnerable, then make me laugh."

Jeff stopped drying her cut.

God, your eyes are beautiful.

Her lips were right there.

"Okay, Hatchett, listen up. I'm going to use your spare T-shirt to wrap around this large band aid I found in the first aid kit in the hall. Hold still." He put the feminine napkin up before she could see it and pressed it against the cut. He had it wrapped in a minute, then had her sit up.

"Hold still. I'll wash your face," Jeff said. "We both got cuts on our head and neck from the tornado."

As he washed her forehead a tear ran down her face. She quickly reached up with one hand and wiped it away.

"Hey, don't mess up my first aid job." Jeff smiled.

Carrie's eyes grew wide, taking in the wood, limbs and debris lying around them at the bottom of the stairs.

"Jeff, we could've been killed. I fell asleep listening to a CD in the library. I missed the announcement, then ran out when I heard the siren start. Thank God you were dumb enough to try to outrun the tornado when I was."

"Yeah, we're lucky, Carrie," said Jeff.

❖❖❖

An hour later, Carrie was listening to the nurse in the draped area for emergency care at the Student Health Center. "You were lucky, honey. It was a good thing your guy knows his first aid. This *Always* brand is a good bandage. He cleaned it well. We'll have a couple of stitches done in a few minutes and we'll get you out of here."

Before Carrie could correct her about Jeff's status in her life, the nurse was gone.

Jeff was looking at the wall.

"Rockhead, you said you had a band aid from a first aid kit!" Carrie said through clenched teeth. "Is that from the women's restroom in Fleener?"

"Yes!" Jeff snapped in a low whisper. "Come down off your indignant rant, queenie. Our medics use feminine napkins instead of a simple band-aid in the field because it absorbs deep cuts better. Okay?!"

Carrie looked at Jeff quietly for several seconds. Tears welled up in her eyes.

"Carrie, I didn't mean to bark at you. I'm sorry…" Jeff trailed off as he leaned back over the gurney.

Carrie put her hand up gently on Jeff's arm. "It's okay. We're good. Just forget that, okay?" She looked away.

"Okay," said Jeff.

Twenty minutes later, they were walking back across campus from the west end toward the Campanile. They walked past yellow crime scene tape, blinking light barriers, and other students walking around to see the damage. Jeff pointed to the route he ran when he thought he was going to run away from it by going to the far side of the library.

From a distance, they could see past the barriers to the emergency lighting they had up next to the Campanile. The top of it had debris damage and one bell was leaning slightly. The base had brick facing stripped off but looked surprisingly sturdy given the hit it had taken. From there, the change in the tornado's path was obvious. It had veered off to the right, came in front of the library, and headed for Fleener Hall as it suddenly turned southeast.

There was the fence post that had just missed Jeff's head, sticking out of the tree like an arrow. The front of Fleener Hall looked the worst of any structure besides the stadium damage.

"We were lucky," Carrie said, looking at the steel post.

"Yeah," said Jeff. "Guess I should take Dave up on a ride next time."

"I'm glad you didn't," said Carrie quietly.

He could have been decapitated and I might have bled to death if...

When they'd left the health center, Jeff had told her he'd walk her to her dorm, then had to get going. They walked without talking. It was the first time they'd ever walked anywhere other than the paths to and from their classes together.

As he walked her up the sidewalk to her dorm, Carrie stopped in front. "Jeff, thanks. You know. For all of it. And this," she said as she gently tapped her 4"x 4" bandage over her stitches.

"We're good, Carrie," said Jeff.

He'd been carrying her backpack since Fleener Hall. He put it on the step, then leaned in and gave her a quick, clumsy hug.

"Take care. And remember what the nurse said about a possible concussion from the blow to the base of the skull," said Jeff. He started to walk away, then turned and grinned at her. "Next time, slow down. It's embarrassing to have a girl outrunning me during a tornado."

Carrie started to laugh, then held the bottom of her neck. "Don't make me laugh. It hurts."

Jeff walked back to his apartment along streets and lawns littered with debris from the tornado. He'd called his folks while Carrie was getting her stitches. He'd calmed down now, realizing how lucky both he and Carrie had been.

I'm okay, he thought. *And, thank God, so is Carrie.*

She saved my life.

17

Loose Ends

MAY 2001

CARRIE LOOKED OUT the back window of the second floor of the library. It had been replaced a week ago, two weeks after the tornado. In the distance, she could see the crane and scaffolding that were up behind the stadium where new electrical boards and a new press box were being installed.

Close and over to the right, the Campanile still stood. "Solid, like an old monument," Dave had said as they walked toward the library earlier.

Most of its damage was in the bell tower and brick/masonry damage near the bottom.

For the first time in years, Carrie had nightmares. She had one where she was running with Jeff but was getting caught up in the vortex of the tornado…and then she'd wake up. Several nights as she drifted to sleep, her last thoughts were a blurry image of Jeff, with his head hovering over her.

We were lucky to survive. Thank God we had each other there that day.

❖❖❖

Websites and hacking, Carrie thought as she saw it was Maureen on her cell. A lot had happened since Maureen Hamilton called her last January to be on the Foundation's Website Task Force with Garrett as chair.

"Carrie, don't say it,' Maureen had laughed. "I know Garrett still has trouble keeping track of his passwords even with your tutoring. But he's an old fraternity brother with Lester Schwerbel. I know Lester's going to try to be his aloof self on this next step, online giving. That's where you come in. We need someone who understands websites and hacking. I think you and Garrett are the best team I can count on to ensure we don't have any problems with its roll out."

With that, Carrie had signed on. The task force meetings had been uneven and uncomfortable for her. She knew Schwerbel as an instructor and he was wary of her presence despite having his own Computer/Info Services staff web specialist, Jerry Mercy, at all the meetings. In late March, they had assured Garrett it had been beta tested and was ready for roll out.

What a fiasco, thought Carrie. *Poor Garrett. He'd trusted Schwerbel.*

"We rolled it out on April Fool's Day. That should have been a caution flag," Garrett had said loudly on the April 13 conference call. It was just Garrett, Lester, Jerry, and Carrie along with Mavis on the line. It had only been up two weeks when its credit card system was hacked and over $6,000 had been lost by donors.

"Lester, I've already had infuriated alums call me directly and chew me out!" yelled Garrett. "You and Jerry assured us it was secure. What happened?"

There was silence for a few seconds, then Jerry stammered, "We, uh, we don't know yet, sir, but I'm working on it."

"Lester, what are you doing to solve this besides having him take the fall?" said Garrett. "I've lost a lot of credibility and some money myself on this hack. What have you lost, so far?"

"Garrett, I'm bringing over another one of our web coordinators to help get to the bottom of this as quickly as we can," said Lester. Carrie could practically feel him sweating through the phone.

"Well, until then, post a message on the website that the online giving system has been closed for upgrades," Garrett said. "Or whatever phrases you use to disguise a hack in your world!"

That short announcement online, a press release, along with Maureen and Garrett's contact to each donor who'd lost money, saved it from being a scandal in the paper. Lester Schwerbel assured

Mavis, Maureen, and Garrett that it would be ready to go back online by September 15, 2001, two weeks before the Foundation's Homecoming meeting and brunch with alumni donors.

"We called each of them and assured them *we* would make good on donations lost if they weren't recovered," Maureen had told Carrie on the phone later. "And we did cover all of the donors' losses personally in May," she added.

◆◆◆

It was a beautiful May afternoon. Much of the damage from the tornado had been cleaned up and repairs were underway across campus. With the north side doorway closed for major repairs, Jeff and Carrie walked out the south side of Fleener.

"Sometimes the government *should* keep secrets longer and better," Jeff said as he stabbed his finger in the air. "I think we have too many leaks to the press that are obviously self-serving for the President, the Vice President, the candidates, a Cabinet member, someone in Congress, or even their congressional aides with clearances."

"I agree," said Carrie.

Jeff looked at her and mockingly acted shocked.

"Yes, Rockhead, we've had too many testosterone and petticoat leaks all through this impeachment circus while we've had two embassies bombed that summer, and now the USS Cole last fall."

Jeff slowed down and looked at Carrie. "What are the times when someone should leak or what's the word...break into a computer system to find information?"

"You mean something like hacking systems?" said Carrie, taking a moment to think about it. "I think we should if it's really important for national defense or some important leader's security. Keeping our information secure from hacking is going to be a much bigger issue when the public realizes how vulnerable our systems are now."

Carrie stopped and turned to look Jeff in the eye. "They may use software hacks to crash a plane or run a ship into the rocks...rather than a missile or suicide bomber."

Jeff looked at her, astonished. "So, would you use your ability to hack to save someone or something if you thought it was a national threat?" he asked.

Carrie looked around to make sure no one was near them. She then leaned closer, and said in a quiet, firm voice, "Hell yes! I hacked the University's grade system last year to make sure I could save my grades and online files in case the old COBOL platform crashed on Y2K *or* it got hacked and crashed."

Jeff looked at Carrie, stunned.

"I can't begin to guess how many policies, rules...LAWS, for Christ sake, that you broke doing that! Why?"

"Because I took COBOL with Schwerbel, the director of the university's computer systems in the fall of '99. He knows COBOL backwards and forwards. But he *doesn't* know how to secure these modern systems from hacking! He's a glorified COBOL programmer who got promoted too far up at the end of that era. Now we're stuck with him as the Director."

"What made you think he couldn't keep us safe for Y2K?" asked Jeff.

"He brought it up in class one day when he was talking proudly about how he had been one of the few programmers who looked ahead to use full four-digit years for code endings. He didn't put in '99, he put in 1999, so it wouldn't get confused with 1899.

"But when Nancy, one of my class friends, asked 'But aren't we also vulnerable from someone hacking in from outside our system to delete the grade system at year end?' Schwerbel got defensive and angry with her. He berated her, and said, 'our system is safe from that. We have solid, fool-proof back doors.'"

Carrie was whispering louder and was more animated now. "A few days later, I found out a freshman I'd been in class with two years ago had hacked our system just to change two C's to A's and make the Dean's list. No one would have caught him except he bragged when he was drunk. They made some secret deal and he transferred."

Carrie looked right at Jeff. "You can never tell ANYONE!" she said. "They'll figure out who told me from the Registrar's office."

"So you hacked your grades before the millennium to ensure they'd be safe?" Jeff asked.

"Yes. And I didn't tell ANYONE," Carrie whispered as she looked at him intensely. "No one in computers. No one from volleyball. Not even my folks or brothers! You're the first one I've EVER told this to, okay?"

Carrie looked away at the Campanile, trying to hide the tears in her eyes.

Jeff gently reached out and touched her arm. "I will never tell anyone. *Anyone.*"

18

Summer 2001

MEMORIAL DAY 2001

"LIZ, IT'S CARRIE. I got off early from Fielding's. I'm going to make it after all."

"Great," said Liz. Light music played in the background. "We're on the deck, just come around back."

"Will do, just want to make a quick call before I come over," said Carrie.

I need to call Brad. We haven't talked for 10 days since I got home. It's been kind of different...since Jeff and I survived the tornado.

His phone went to voice mail after one ring. *That's weird. Brad usually goes to voice mail after four rings...but he always picks up my calls on the first three rings if he's not busy.*

Carrie finished getting ready, went out to the car, and decided to call again.

On the third ring, Brad answered. There was a muffled sound of laughter, giggling, and *Lady Marmalade* blaring in the background.

"Hey, Carrie. Good to hear from you. How's your Memorial Day?"

"Getting better. I got off early from Fielding's so I'm going over to a deck party at Liz's. How's yours going, Bradley? Sounds like fun in the background."

"Oh, yeah, it's just the Memorial Day dance at River Park," said Brad, still muffled.

"BRAD STIPPICK. Get your ass back over here and dance with me some more!"

Brad's phone suddenly had no noise in the background. A couple seconds later, he was back on.

"Sorry, Carrie, that's just someone that came with Greg's little sister tonight. She thinks my name is Stippick."

Carrie was quiet on the other end.

"Carrie, I'm in my car now. I'm sorry. It's too loud out there."

"Well," said Carrie, "I don't want to interrupt a good time."

The line was quiet on the other end.

"Carrie, I was going to call you. I'm sorry we're talking about this now. It's been different this last month…since the tornado. That was pretty traumatic. You seemed to be somewhere else when we were out…not always there. I, well…I still want to get together sometime this summer but I wondered if…

"We should date others for the summer if we want?" said Carrie, trying not to have a catch in her voice.

"Well, yeah," said Brad. "Now that you put it that way. Carrie, there's no OTHER woman. I just…"

"Brad, I think that's probably a good idea. I may do that, too. Let's get together this summer if we can but be…okay for now."

"Okay, Carrie. Take care."

As Carrie was hanging up, she heard a quick, "I love you."

Tears welled up in her eyes as she drove to Liz's party.

"Hanging on a Moment" by Lifehouse came on the radio.

Brad, I still love you, but I can't keep hanging on a moment for you. No spinster's life this summer. Time to just let life happen.

◆◆◆

IVAN'S TRYING TO HACK US

"Carrie, be careful you don't step on toes," her mom, Betty, had said on the drive to her first day that morning. "I've worked, had lunch, and socialized with Fred and a lot of these folks for years." Carrie's summer internship at Westham Energy was mainly due to her mom's work as Executive Assistant to the CEO.

"I know, Mom," said Carrie respectfully. "I

will." Truthfully, she was still intimidated by her mom's boss, John Hartman, the CEO.

Carrie had gone there with her mom one Saturday when she was 13. She 'shadowed' with the computer operators while her mom finished a project.

Hartman had walked by the computer operations window and stopped. His look chilled her. Several minutes later, her mom came, thanked the operators for the favor, and took Carrie back to the office. She stayed in a chair next to her mom for the next hour, reading power journals. Later when her mom let Hartman know she was finished, she said, "Sorry about Carrie visiting the computer department."

◆◆◆

"Well, Carrie," said Fred, the Director of Computer Services, "after you finish your sit down with Bonnie and each supervisor and their specialists in each unit, get back to me.

"We need a fresh set of eyes for our system security. Someone with modern classroom and online experience," Fred said with a straightforward but somewhat embarrassed look on his face.

"Experts warned us to learn and keep up with means of detecting attempted hacks into our systems and grids."

"Carrie, here's the seminar's checklist on checking for hacking attempts," Fred said as he opened the folder.

This is a boiler-plate from my class a year ago,

thought Carrie. *Good, they admit they have to get with the times.*

The checklist included:

1. Were there any hacking attempts they were not aware of?
2. Can they track them or source them?
3. What could be done to make their "back doors," of their systems more secure?
4. Did they need to have just some more patches, new software, or a new system?

Well, knowing the right questions to ask is easy, thought Carrie. *I've got confidence on checking back doors, but finding hack attempts and being able to tell what source their code is…that's going to be new turf.*

Okay, I wanted to be challenged and stretch. Time to step up.

❖❖❖

"Carrie, I've got to be open with you about changes," said Bonnie, a senior programmer at lunch that day in the cafeteria with her mom. "With this new open sourcing, we don't know *what we don't know!* We've got to defend our business in the public's interest. These are high stakes."

❖❖❖

"There it is," Carrie whispered to herself in her corner cube. "Damn, there were some bad boys here."

The first was the common weak password situation. But disturbingly, she also found some attempts at being hacked the previous fall that the lead for website administration had not identified. It was deep inside their code.

Really Fred!? Thought Carrie. *You used your three kids' first and last initials and their years of birth for the backdoor password! No symbols or punctuation marks for added strength? I read this in the employees' Spot Light newsletter Mom brought home last Christmas. Homer Simpson could come up with these. DOH!*

"Bonnie, this hack attempt was hidden in a strange code," Carrie told her. "I don't recognize it from common nationals, internationals, and rogue hackers we've studied or that I can find online. Can I make some long distance calls here and some on my cell for research?"

"Yes, definitely," Bonnie said. "I've woken up more than one night wondering what an international one would look like. I wouldn't know."

Carrie's *Computer & Website System Security* class had been taught by the best and youngest information systems instructor, Assistant Professor Karen Perrick. She had a section on computer hacking that was both fascinating and scary. Karen attended the *Def Con* hackers' convention in Vegas each summer.

"Folks, imagine a bunch of pimply-faced

teenagers working on their laptops furiously at one table," Professor Perrick said dryly in class. "At an adjacent table, FBI agents sit, conspicuous in their new jeans and polo shirts. They are trying to listen to two of the young hackers describe how they want to emulate the teen who'd hacked the Defense and NASA sites last year. It caused the International Space Station computers to shut down."

Carrie decided to call Karen back at FSU and shared the strange code language. Karen said it was new to her too but said she'd get back to Carrie after Def Con in early July.

Two weeks later on Friday afternoon, Karen called from Vegas. "Carrie, I've got some unsettling news. This has the markings of the newest group of Russian hackers," Karen said and paused.

"Promise me you'll be careful with these guys. Some are definitely rogues but some work indirectly for the Russian government under the guise of mavericks.

"According to a younger FBI agent I befriended here, there's also a third group. It is probably the most dangerous one to call out if you find their code.

"They are guarded by the Russian mob, Carrie, okay?" said Karen.

Carrie closed her eyes and felt a chill run down her spine. She felt the terror that she did when she ran out of the library during the tornado that spring.

"That movie a few years ago, *The Saint*, is part

science fiction on the cold fusion, but the violent power struggles going on in Russia are very real. There are ongoing battles right now, real and financial, with the oligarchs grabbing power. Both President Yeltsin and the one that recently got elected, Putin, hated it, but they had to deal with them. Rumor has it that they even paid them cyber ransom several times. These guys are cutting edge on this new front. They are fearless and ruthless in their cyber extortion."

Carrie got off the phone. She leaned forward, studying the code trail. She looked up blankly at the wall of her back corner cube. Her fear became a slow, burning anger.

Ivan's trying to hack us.

◆◆◆

"Carrie, Clint here. Hope you got my messages. Can we go out again sometime? Just give me a call, okay?"

It was Clint Phillips' third voice mail this week.

Take the hint, Clint, thought Carrie as she dropped her cell on the bed.

Clint Phillips, high-school all-star quarterback. I used to pine for the idea of you holding me. What a disappointment you are…to yourself. Couldn't believe you were finally interested in me when I saw you at Liz's 4th of July party. You're finally interested in me after all these years and we go out.

Smart choice on movie for our first date. Took me

to A.I., Artificial Intelligence instead of Fast & Furious, she thought as she stepped into the shower. *A surprising night. You'd learned how to listen. You were smart not to try that night.*

Next date, dinner at Fielding's. You knew what you were doing there. Letting me know you were honored, not afraid to show that YOU were out with Carrie Station, the late bloomer. The conditioner began to rinse out.

You made me feel special, beautiful…desirable. I wanted to know how it would feel. To be with you. The warm water continued to wash over her. *Going out to your brother's cabin was perfect for that.*

You were such a disappointment. Didn't have the sweetness or gentle timing of Brad. Didn't say or whisper anything to me. We must have been done in five minutes. In the car on the way home, didn't say anything.

Nope, you're just not my type of man. Not headed anywhere. Not really sensitive or caring. Brad and I may have drifted into dating others this summer, but he beats you any day of the week. You don't know how to make a woman really laugh and love you. Love herself. Like Jeff…Jeff.

Carrie turned the shower off quickly. Dried off and dressed fast.

She got to Tim and Christine's by 6:30 to babysit for "Mom and Dad's date night," so they could see *The Fast and The Furious.*

Later, as she tucked Zach into bed, she kissed him and said, "You know, you're my kind of guy."

◆ ◆ ◆

"Carrie, you'd better get with Bonnie and set up a meeting first thing tomorrow with Fred." Her mom looked solemn over breakfast on Sunday. "I don't know where this world's going. You be careful what you do for your own safety, okay?"

"I will, Mom," said Carrie. "Karen told me not to do or say anything in chat rooms, post anything, or do letters to the editor. They won't know it's me…or us, if we just tighten the backdoor on the system."

"Okay, but know this. We're so proud of you. Maureen Hamilton put you on a task force with Garrett Hamilton for the Foundation's website. Aunt Harriet still can't get over that."

Mom's never admitted she resents her older sister for being a snoot. Wow.

◆ ◆ ◆

"Why in the hell would the Russian mob want to break into our regional utility out here in the Midwest?" Fred asked after Carrie had briefed him.

"From what Professor Perrick says from these Def Con events, it's their style to hack, to copy or take some vital material, but not shut your system down," Carrie said cautiously. "They're ruthless mercenaries. They'll sell our hack to the highest bidder, IF they get in. Luckily, they didn't make it last fall but they, or someone else, will if we don't harden our passwords and security for our whole system."

◆◆◆

"Fred and Carrie, this is Agent Frank Murdock, a cyber specialist from the Chicago field office of the FBI," said John Hartman as he motioned for them to have a seat.

Murdock stood up. He was 5'11", an inch shorter than Carrie, even with her obligatory flats on. Dark suit, light blue oxford button down, and conservative burgundy tie. And a hard, overdone grip for a handshake.

These shorter alpha males and their overkill handshakes, thought Carrie. *Must be trying to compensate for size.*

"Ms. Station, in the report we received from your CEO, you recommended that this unsuccessful attempt at hacking Westham's computer and grid system may have been an affiliate of the Russian mob. Why?"

What an ass, thought Carrie. *He thinks he'll intimidate me when I'm more worried about the Russian mob?*

She looked at Fred. He nodded.

Carrie pointed at a thick computer read out. "This forensic trail of code is why."

She opened it to the pages of highlighted code lines. "These 12 have been identified as independent and 'gaming' hackers who tried to hack Westham. All were unsuccessful."

Looking directly at Murdock, Carrie said, "As you already know, three have been identified as local community college freshmen who were "invited down" to the federal court house for a visit with a local FBI agent and the District Attorney."

Murdock's jaws tightened as John Hartman and Fred both looked at him with surprised, aggravated expressions.

Carrie continued looking at Murdock. "The students had a late night contest to see who could hack Westham Utility first and cause a power failure. One of them got in through the back door but was stopped by our firewall."

Carrie then pointed to the one she'd marked in light green. "This is the one we suspect of being the Russian mob's hacker because of the end wording he/they used on their code. Its syntax is backward in several places and they use 'chi_d_set' for their end tag."

"What makes you think that's Russian Mob?" Murdock snapped.

"Because that's what one of them bragged about during a break to my computer professor at *Def Con* in Vegas earlier this summer. He laughed that it turned attention toward the Chinese since they had been the bad boys of human rights with the last administration.

That too deep for you, Barney Fife? Carrie thought.

"Ivan is trying to hack us," Carrie said in a flourish that she immediately regretted.

Murdock gave Carrie a cold stare. "So you know about the *Def Con* hacking convention?" Murdock asked.

Hartman gave Carrie a slight nod and tight smile that Murdock didn't see.

"Yes, sir. Most computer geeks and IT majors in US colleges know about it by the end of their freshman year. Some consider it an advanced computer camp," said Carrie.

Murdock glowered at Carrie.

If Garrett Hamilton gave me that look, I'd be scared, thought Carrie. *But you are out of your league.*

John Hartman broke the silence. "Agent Murdock, have you seen coding and hacking attempts with this specific set of letters and sequence? Are we wrong?"

Murdock gave Hartman a flustered look. Carrie clasped her hands underneath the conference table to keep from showing her shaking hands.

"No, but I'll take this print out back to the FBI computer forensics lab to see what they think," said Murdock as he began to pull the two-page perforated print out toward his folder.

"Sir, we'll need to copy those before we let you take our findings and notes back," said Carrie.

Murdock gave Hartman a stern look. Hartman met Murdock with a smile and frozen look.

"Yes, here, be sure to keep your own copy to compare with any future hacking attempts by this source. You'll let us know if you receive any others," Murdock said as he looked at Fred rather than Carrie.

"Here are the originals, Agent Murdock," Carrie said with a smile as she slid them across the boardroom table a few minutes later.

John Hartman adjourned the meeting, thanked him for his visit, and then added, "Agent Murdock, I'll let both our senators and the governor know how much we appreciated your special trip out here to help us with this problem."

Murdock gave John and Fred a businesslike smile as he shook their hands. When he got to Carrie, he gave her a short, hard handshake with a tight smile and said, "Good work finding this code, Ms. Station. We'll see who sent this."

Fred escorted Murdock to the front security door.

John Hartman turned and said, "Good work, Carrie. This is serious and you found it, not their forensics lab." Then with a smile, he added, "Go easy on the feds when you embarrass them. They find a way to 'gig' you later."

"Yes, Mr. Hartman," blurted Carrie. "I didn't mean to reflect badly on you or Westham, sir."

"You didn't. He had that coming," Hartman said as they walked out by her mom's desk. "Their FBI director that just stepped down last month had them take the computer OFF his desk eight years ago. They missed Hansen spying for Russia for over 15 years. The US has a ways to come back from that FBI leadership and what was missed. They could learn something from you."

Hartman winked at her as he walked away.

Carrie turned around, relieved.

Carrie noticed her mom looking at her like she never had before, like she was seeing Carrie in a different light. Carrie felt different too, like she'd just gone through an amazing rite of passage.

She walked back to her cubicle, looked back, and saw the proud look on her mom's face.

◆◆◆

HE'S GOT A HIT OUT ON US

"Well, are you two 'The Twins' who are so great at intervals?" asked First Sgt. Fernandez.

Smitty froze. Jeff grinned. "Yes, First Sgt. Fernandez. Did First Sgt. Florence tell you what good soldiers we were, too?"

"No, not quite," Fernandez said, peering down over his glasses through their Humvee window. He paused. "But he said you improved last summer. Said to say hi."

Fernandez continued down the line of the convoy with his clipboard.

Smitty exhaled. "Hanford, you and your cheesy grin are gonna get us in trouble or whooped in a bar some night! We're headed for the land of cheese. You oughta fit right in."

They were at Scott Air Force Base in Belleville, Illinois. They were helping unload and transport equipment, troops, and fuel as part of a large joint transport/lift exercise that had brought equipment back from Kuwait.

It was the 10th year of the US/Allies deploying active and air guard wings for the Iraq No-Fly Zone.

◆◆◆

Three hours later, they were on the interstate, headed toward Camp McCoy. They had just crossed over the border into Wisconsin.

"So this is the land of cheese and God's country," Smitty said with a grin. "We make Caterpillars in Peoria and don't claim to be from God's country!"

"I know," said Jeff. "My girlfriend's from downstate Illinois, too. She says she gets tired of Chicago always claiming they're the center of the world…and, oh yeah, the US too."

"Hey, how is it with you two?" teased Smitty. "You got the engagement ring yet?"

"No. Don't you start too," Jeff laughed, pointing at Smitty. "The last two months of school were lovey dovey one day, then jealous the next."

"JEALOUS! You been sneaking around on the side, Choir Boy?" screeched Smitty.

"No. No. NO!" said Jeff angrily. "It's just that

there is this girl, Carrie, I've known for over a year. We got caught in the tornado in April."

"And? And? And…" Smitty said, snapping his fingers over at Jeff. "What are you holdin' back?"

"Carrie's a beautiful brunette, six foot tall," said Jeff, looking out at the green rolling hills. "A volleyball star who wears her hair in a ponytail with a sweat shirt and blue jeans every day in history classes. Then we have this dress-up brunch last fall and she shows up with red lipstick and this gorgeous dress on her incredible body…"

"HANFORD! The Tornado!" yelled Smitty above the road noise and wind coming through the open windows.

"Okay. The tornado," Jeff said, turning his gaze to the Army gas truck 300 feet ahead. "She and Dave and I have become good friends in class. I tease her a lot. She hates it and loves it. I talk to her about stuff that I can't talk to Amy about. Carrie gets history, people's feelings. *And she respects the military*!" Jeff yelped as he pointed back at Smitty triumphantly.

Smitty was looking back at him as he drove. He calmly yelled over the noise, "So what happened in the tornado, Jeff?"

"I stupidly tried to outrun it. She missed the tornado warning on the loudspeaker. Asleep in the library with her earphones on," Jeff yelled back. "I came running around the far side of the library as she ran out the front of it. She yelled at me to duck a fence post that would have taken my head off. Saved my life.

"I picked her up after a flying tree limb knocked her down, nearly out, on the steps of a building. I got her inside, down to the basement just as the tornado blew the windows in behind us. Maybe I saved her life."

Jeff reached into the glove compartment for their *Always* "bandage" pack in the first aid kit and held it up. "I treated her gash on her neck with one of these. Then we just laid there holding each other until the worst was over." He remembered the feeling of her head against his chest, how close their faces were…and her brown eyes.

Smitty was silent a few seconds, then turned to Jeff. He shook his head sympathetically. "You're in love with two women, Hanford."

"NO! It was just something that happened," Jeff yelled, looking back. "It was one of those traumatic life events, like combat."

"Like combat. LIKE COMBAT!" Smitty laughed. "You save me in combat, I'm gonna' like you a lot, Hanford. But I ain't gonna MARRY YOU!"

Smitty kept laughing. Jeff just turned and looked at the road ahead.

◆ ◆ ◆

That night, Smitty and Jeff had their rig, tents, and showers squared away by 2000 hours. They walked down to the end of the row of vehicles and tents on the grass. First Sgt. Fernandez was there at a picnic table and waved them over.

"Smitty and Hanford, say hello to First Sgt. Flood," Fernandez said, pointing toward Flood. "He helped get these rigs onboard to fly back from Kuwait. He and I go back to the Gulf War 10 years ago. Take a load off if you want ONE beer each."

"Thanks, Top. Good to meet you, First Sergeant," Smitty said as he shook hands. Jeff followed suit and they soon had a beer from God's country.

"How long were you there for the load prep and transport loading, Top?" Jeff asked First Sgt. Flood.

"Too long. It was a week, seemed like two," said Flood as he leaned on his knee with a foot up on the picnic table seat. "Haven't been that scared since we went through the berm to start Desert Storm in '91."

He looked at Fernandez. "We were ordered to stay inside of the concertina wire of the compound for the whole week. Out in the middle of that Kuwaiti desert next to that airbase."

"We've got Saddam pretty well corralled and contained. What's got them so spooked?" asked Fernandez.

"It's Osama. Word from the intel chatter is that he's got a hit out on us," replied Flood.

19

Back for the Last Year

LATE AUGUST 2001

QUITE A SUMMER after all, thought Carrie while she drove back to FSU. *I was afraid I'd just be a bored intern and babysit Zach for my male companionship.*

I hope Jeff had a good summer training at Guard camp, thought Carrie as the Campanile and FSU campus came into site in the distance. *He'll need it if Amy goes on a jealous rant again.*

◆ ◆ ◆

Carrie was unpacking in the new apartment she, Amber, and Erin had rented for their senior year when her phone rang.

"Carrie, it's Maureen. How was your summer?"

Oh, if only I could tell you. You know more about the men in my life than my mom.

"The internship at Westham was good, a great experience," said Carrie. "My folks are good."

"You'll find that more now, honey," said Maureen. "I grew wistful my final year and realized how much my folks had meant to me in my journey."

Maureen talks to me like a daughter sometimes, thought Carrie warmly. *Poor gal had two boys and Garrett.*

"Garrett and I got in to the Holiday Inn early this afternoon," said Maureen. "Garrett would like to ask you something before tomorrow morning's Website Task Force meeting. Here he is."

"Hi Carrie," said Garrett in that quiet but commanding baritone voice. "Sounds like your summer was good."

"Yes it was, but it's great to be back. Senior year!"

"I know. We really appreciate all you've done for FSU and us," Garrett said, then flowed right into his question.

"We were wondering if you'd be able to join us for dinner here in the room tonight? I'd like to talk to you before the breakfast meeting tomorrow morning."

"Well, yes, I can," said Carrie. "I can't get out there until 7:00 p.m. Is that all right?"

"Yes, that will be great. And can you bring your laptop?" He had hung up before he waited for the answer.

He's smooth, thought Carrie. *Gets away with a command sounding like a request every time.*

Now to let Brad know our date's off until Saturday night. He'll live. Probably at the Hofhaus!

◆ ◆ ◆

It was the first time Carrie had had a dinner in their room at the hotel. They'd previously eaten in the restaurant downstairs but tonight, the privacy of just Maureen, Garrett and she alone was flattering and felt good.

She arrived 15 minutes early to their suite. They sat down at the circular table by the balcony while they began the room service dinner. The late summer sun washed in through the curtains.

"Carrie, this is delicate, but I've got to be direct on a question," said Garrett.

"You're worried about my sex life with the football star?" Carrie said, then immediately covered her mouth.

Garrett's face flushed. Seconds went by, then the plate glass table reverberated with a THWAK from Maureen hitting it.

"Oh, God, what I'd give to have a picture of your face!" Maureen laughed hysterically at Garrett.

"Oh, Governor, I'm SO sorry!" Carrie burst out. "I chugged a can of Coke on the way out to wake up."

Garrett's face was flustered. Then he started to laugh with Maureen, who'd nearly chocked on her salad.

"He's never had a daughter," Maureen said, giggling. "That would have been his face at the dinner table if he'd had a blunt daughter.

Garrett chuckled. "Yes. A daughter would probably have been my princess and pushed all my buttons."

I can't believe that just happened, that I said that. Maureen. Garrett. And me.

"Okay, Garrett, get back to the website," said Maureen. She winked at Carrie.

"Yes, the Foundation's website," said Garrett, regaining his composure. "Can you hack it?"

Carrie froze. She finally looked up from her salad.

"Even if I could, why?" Carrie asked slowly as she met Garrett's gaze.

"Because Lester Schwebel's put the Foundation, the University, and us in an intolerable situation," said Garrett angrily. "I don't trust his assurances anymore. And I'm not including the money Maureen and I personally paid back to donors."

Maureen's eyes widened as she looked at Garrett.

"Come on, Maureen, I know you call Carrie on your own. You've calmed or parted the waters for me like that for years." He gave Maureen a warm smile. "And saved me."

"Garrett, it's against the law and University policy," Carrie said as she looked him squarely in the eye. "I'd be expelled, have a felony or jail time, and no future."

"Not if the President of the University has approved it with my request," Garrett said nonchalantly as he finished his bite of salad.

"Hack the Foundation's website with the President's approval." Carrie exhaled as she put her hands in her lap.

"Carrie, we wouldn't ask you if we both didn't feel Lester Schwerbel was leaving someone high and dry again. It's his nature," Maureen said, her voice icy. "He left a girl friend of mine in an indefensible situation during our senior year and walked away."

Carrie sat and looked at her lap, quietly processing one more reason she didn't like Schwerbel.

"That's completely confidential, Carrie," Garrett said, returning his gaze to her.

"Will you do it?"

Carrie looked at Maureen, then Garrett.

"Yes. With one more ground rule," said Carrie, giving them both a solemn look. "You can't look over my shoulder or stand behind me. You can never be cornered with a question that you'd seen this or any other website get hacked. Got it?"

"I'll get my laptop out."

Ten minutes later, Carrie turned to Maureen and Garrett. They were sitting on their bed on the other side of the suite, holding hands.

They look like parents with a daughter "in trouble."

Carrie cleared her throat. "I'm in. They strengthened the back door but I wouldn't trust them with Westham Energy's grid."

◆◆◆

"Help yourselves to the coffee and pastries," said Garrett Hamilton as he shook hands with Lester Schwerbel and Jerry Mercy. "Thanks for coming in on a Saturday morning."

Carrie was the only other one there. She'd asked Garrett to meet her early to set up the laptop quietly on a table over in the corner. Their table for eight with food was the only other set up. It was in the middle of the small breakout room in the back of the Holiday Inn.

"Since this is a meeting of a minority of the Website Task Force, there will be no minutes," said Garrett, looking around the table at the other three.

"There's no written agenda," Garrett continued. "We all know we're here to talk about the Foundation's website integrity and being ready for it to go live again for online donations on September 15. Right?"

"Yes," said Lester, after he looked at a somber Jerry Mercy.

"Is the Foundation Website secure right now on its backdoor before we finalize the credit card security functions?" Garrett asked as he looked back and forth between Lester and Jerry.

Good man, Garrett. Got the phrase right. We'll work on the five-dollar words later.

"Yes," Lester said in an aggravated tone as Garrett pointed at him.

"Yes," said Jerry in a dry voice.

"Good," said Garrett as he got up and waved his hand toward the laptop on the table in the corner. "Let's go check it out."

Jerry's face went ashen. Lester looked angry, his jaw set as he walked over behind Garrett. Carrie followed behind, nervously trying to unclench her fists.

"Carrie, would you bring up the Foundation's website, please," Garrett asked in his 'command as request' voice.

Carrie took a seat and opened the laptop with the website already on the screen. She hit refresh. Lester stood directly behind her, Jerry to his left. Garrett leaned against the wall, facing Carrie.

"Carrie, open up its back door. Hack it, if you can," Garrett commanded.

Carrie was into the Foundation's website and through its backdoor in three minutes.

"I want to know how she did that!" said Lester through gritted teeth. "And she's going to give Jerry the documentation on the path she used. Then I'm going to talk to the President about this intrusion."

Garrett looked at Lester coldly and replied, "Lester, we did this with the President's blessing and request.

"Maureen and I are having dinner at the President's

house tonight. We'll talk about what *we* recommend from this experience and for the University's future computer and online security."

Well, that was terrifying. Let's see if I survive my senior year as an information systems major.

Carrie closed her laptop. "I'll get the documentation with code to Mr. Schwerbel, Jerry, you, and Maureen, if you like, Governor."

"That's sounds good for confidentiality and accountability," said Garrett, returning Lester's glare.

"And, Lester," Garrett said as he pointed his finger, "Get this straight. There will be no retribution, no retaliation by YOU or anyone against Carrie for this." He continued jabbing his finger at Lester. "It's to be kept secret for the University's sake, the Foundation's sake, and all of our sakes. UNDERSTOOD?"

He kept his finger pointed at Lester until he said, "Yes," in a low, resigned tone.

"Yes," said Jerry immediately when Garrett pointed toward him.

"Yes," said Carrie as Garrett lowered his finger and looked down at her.

"I'll let the President get back to you on what will be done next," Garrett said to Lester as he motioned for Carrie to pack up. "We're through here."

The next Monday, as classes were starting, Lester Schwerbel agreed to the President's assignment of an outside website consulting firm to confidentially work to ensure the University's computer and online security.

◆◆◆

"Thanks Brad," Carrie said as they walked out of "Summer Catch" at The Metro. "It was lightweight relief. That's what I needed."

"Yeah, I was afraid you'd want "War and Peace" at some encore series at the Commons," Brad said with a wink.

Carrie laughed as they walked toward his car.

"Go to the Hofhaus?" Brad asked.

"No, not there," Carrie said holding up her hand. "I've had a long day. No karaoke tonight, okay?"

"How about my place?" Brad said. "My roommates are gone for the night."

"Well, how convenient," Carrie said in her high nasal Church Lady voice. "Our Little Bradley Kippick has the place all to himself tonight. Well, isn't that special."

Brad had stopped walking. He was shaking his head, laughing. Carrie had done Church Lady one night last winter when she'd had too much to drink at one of his friend's parties. She had launched into "Little Bradley Kippick, with that gorgeous, bulbous behind that all the strumpets on campus just love to watch run down the field. Isn't he special? Run Bradley, run."

Everyone loved it, Brad the most. It was during the height of their relationship. They were in love.

No one could take Brad Kippick down a peg better than Carrie. But she never did Church Lady on Brad again. Until tonight.

"What brought her back?" asked Brad as he straightened up.

"Punchy, I think," Carrie said as she laughed at breaking up Brad. "A little sentimental, too. Let's go to your place. I'd like to get away tonight."

♦♦♦

"Carrie, I'm sorry about that phone call Memorial Day and how clumsy I was at saying I wanted to date around," said Brad.

Carrie was lying next to him in bed. They'd made love after they'd gotten back to his apartment.

She held her hand up in the dark.

"Brad, it's okay. I was actually in the same place, but in denial about what I was feeling."

Well, time for the truth.

Carrie continued, looking at the ceiling as she talked in the late night darkness of the apartment.

"Later, I had a fling with the high school all-star quarterback I had a crush on in high school. He finally realized I was beautiful but 'didn't know it' or some line like that."

Carrie poked Brad's leg under the sheet. He chortled, then slapped both of his hands on his face melodramatically.

"Oh my God! A QUARTERBACK! Was he better than me?" Brad croaked.

Carrie couldn't stop laughing and punched Brad's shoulder as he continued to hold his face, laughing.

Carrie lay back down on her pillow. After a few seconds, she quietly said, "No he wasn't. He's stuck in high school, inconsiderate, and isn't going anywhere.

"Brad, you're a good man. Hear me?" Carrie said as she reached over and held his hand under the covers.

"Thanks," Brad said with a catch in his throat. "It's over, isn't it?"

"Yes," Carrie said as she quietly cried. "I'm sorry."

"Don't be," Brad said with a short squeeze of her hand. "I knew I was in love with you at the Variety Show last fall. Not because of the catch and the game.

"I felt so lucky to be walking in there…with you. Not Carrie Station the volleyball star but Carrie, the drop dead beautiful, tall, sexy woman with a killer sense of humor and smarter than Einstein."

"Easy, cowboy," Carrie laughed. "You kind of have me on a pedestal there."

"Both the brains and the looks?" chortled Brad.

"No, just the brains. You had me believing the beauty part after the stop and the kiss that first night." She squeezed his hand, trying to stop her tears.

They both lay quietly for several minutes.

"Last fall was like riding a romantic rocket on steroids," said Carrie. "And I loved it. And I'll always have a place in my heart for you. You were my first real love. I guess I'm a late bloomer with a weak spot for football studs."

They both laughed and held hands tight again.

"Carrie, you're so special," Brad said. "I don't know what it will be, but you're going to do things that the rest of us won't even be able to understand. Like Jeff says, you can dumb it down for us pedestrians and make it work."

"You and Jeff Hanford talk?" Carrie asked in a low voice.

"Yeah, Jeff and I are drinking buddies at times," Brad mumbled.

Brad and Rockhead drinking buddies. How big and how small my world has been this last year.

Brad drifted to sleep against her shoulder. She lay there for more than an hour but couldn't sleep.

Carrie rolled over gently and kissed Brad's forehead.

Good-bye Brad. You loved me and helped me to love myself. I'll always be thankful to you for that.

The Hofhaus was quiet as she walked past at 3:00 in the morning. Up the hill, the Campanile's bells chimed three times with that beautiful clanging melody.

I did my internship, told off an FBI jerk in front of my mom's boss, had a fling with the high school crush, hacked the university's website with the president's and former governor's blessings...and broke it off with my first real love. That's enough for one summer.

I'm ready to get back to normal.

20

9/11

TUESDAY, SEPTEMBER 11, 2001

LIKE MUCH OF the Midwest, it was an Indian summer day on the FSU campus. Temperature in the mid-60's with few clouds in a blue sky. The flag by the library flapped gently from a soft, southerly breeze.

"Hanford, I don't know why I let you talk me into taking this *Modern Middle East History*," said Dave. He held up his textbook. "They're big as phone books and as dense. I should have put it off for grad school sometime down the road."

"Sorry, I didn't see this load coming either," said Jeff. "But, three months from this Friday, we'll be done. Get a coffee with me in the Union?"

"No, had my Venti Sumatra already," Dave said with a grin and his eyes opened wide. He took the steps up over the Union while Jeff went in the door below him.

"Hey, Jeff, coming for your fix too?" said Carrie as she was walking into the Coffee Bar.

"Morning, Carrie," said Jeff, joining her in line. "Yeah, gotta' feed the habit. Just saw Dave. He's giving me grief about my 'urging him' to take *Modern Middle East History* in case Uncle Sam chooses to send us for an 'extended studies tour' over there."

"This class IS a load," said Carrie, glaring at him. "I don't know how I let you talk me into it. I should have forced Dave to be my advisor instead of you, Rockhead."

"Yeah, yeah." The TV on the wall above caught his attention. "Hey, what's this?" Jeff said, motioning to the TV.

The twin towers were on the screen with the one on the right trailing black smoke out of a bizarrely shaped big black gash in its side. Across the screen at the bottom was the title "World Trade Center." Up above was a little box with "LIVE."

Carrie turned after paying for her coffee. "That's one of the Twin Towers on fire. How did it get so big? It's so black."

"Hey, can you turn that TV up?" Jeff asked the manager working near the TV. She looked up, then stood transfixed by the scene.

Soon, several in line behind Jeff said, "Turn it up. Turn it up, PLEASE!"

"Let's go out to the jumbo news screen," said Jeff as he waited for his coffee. He turned to see Carrie already curling out to the large dining area.

"I'm not going to class yet," Carrie said when Jeff reached her.

"Me either," he said as they kept their eyes on the jumbo screen. Within five minutes, there were over 50 students standing in the corner amongst the café tables, chairs, and walkway. No one was seated.

"I don't think this is a plane accident," Jeff said. She looked at him silently.

"Oh, my God!" screamed a young woman behind them.

They looked up to see the north tower with a huge fireball shooting out of it sideways, billowing out into a perfect blue sky.

Carrie gasped and grabbed Jeff's wrist. Neither spoke. Then a replay from a different angle showed a second plane coming in at a slant from the right before hitting the north tower.

"Jeff, this is our Pearl Harbor," Carrie whispered so only he could hear. "But it's here, hitting Manhattan this time."

Jeff turned and looked at Carrie while she kept her eyes on the screen.

"Carrie, you're connecting the dots and making the analogy again."

Carrie and Jeff watched and talked in shock for the next 30 minutes in a surreal, tragic world they could not stop watching as it played out on national TV, live. Dave had worked his way into the crowd, standing next to Jeff.

"I called Guard headquarters," said Dave. "They said to stop calling. They'll call us on the 'stand by or come in ASAP' robo-call if needed."

A hollow feeling like when he saw the tornado come out of the trees came over Jeff.

"Thanks, I hadn't thought that far ahead," said Jeff. "How the hell did this happen!"

Carrie shook her head as she looked past Jeff to Dave. All around them, people were crying, swearing, or standing in disbelief, just trying to make sense of the surreal scenes on the screen. For most there was no way to make sense of it. Strangers and friends hugged each other, looking for comfort.

Suddenly, the TV showed a different site. Smoke filled the screen. Below it was the title: "The Pentagon."

"Shit, they've hit D.C., too!" Dave said in startled voice. Carrie gasped and muffled a scream.

"Osama has a hit out on us," Jeff said, his jaw clenched. "Flood thought it was overseas…we all thought it was overseas. They're hitting us here, at home. And they're using our own planes."

Carrie watched as many students and faculty around them turned to look at Jeff.

He'd announced something they weren't hearing on national TV. Several started murmuring while they stared at Jeff as if they were looking to him for answers.

Reading their minds, Jeff spoke up, "One of our first sergeants came home from Kuwait in July and told us he was scared. He said, and I'm quoting, 'Osama has a hit out on us.' We all thought it was meant for overseas embassies, military bases, and ships like the USS Cole in Yemen last year. Folks, the terrorists are bringing a war HERE to America."

Most who'd turned now looked at Jeff in awe. He'd surprised himself by delivering a speech in public as if he did it every day. And many around him looked at him like he was a commander, a leader.

Carrie's face was wet with tears as she looked at him.

"I hope they don't take you and Dave," she whispered through her tears.

◆◆◆

About 20 minutes later, there was a report that a fourth plane was missing and there were reports of smoke coming from a field near Shanksville, Pennsylvania.

About 30 minutes later, the North Tower collapsed.

As it collapsed with a second horrific round of clouds of smoke and debris blowing through the streets of Manhattan, Dave quietly said to Jeff, "Like the scene from *Independence Day*." Jeff looked down at the floor beside Dave and sadly nodded.

The magnitude of the attacks had overwhelmed everyone in the union.

Jeff felt a foreboding of war coming into his life.

Carrie slowly pivoted in front of Jeff and Dave. She had tears in her eyes.

"Okay, guys," she said in a shaky voice. "You've got my cell. You call me if you get called in by the Guard, okay?" she said, looking at Dave, then Jeff.

"Gotcha, Carrie," said Dave solemnly.

"Will do," said Jeff grimly.

Carrie stepped forward, gently grasped each of their elbows, pulled them toward her, laid her head down between their shoulders, and choked, "God, please keep these two safe." She pulled back, turned, and was gone before either could say anything.

◆ ◆ ◆

"Carrie, I don't believe how many are here," said Amber. It was 3:00 p.m. After the announcement that classes at FSU were suspended for the remainder of the day, many had gone back to their dorms or apartments and continued watching TV as they called home, talked to roommates, or walked the halls seeking others.

"You made a good call," said Amber. "This is something we can do as a team today."

They were at the local blood bank near the mall. 15 of the FSU women's volleyball team had come out in several cars and the coach's minivan. They were all in their royal blue travel sweats with hair done and make up on.

Initially Amber seemed put off when Carrie phoned the team earlier in the morning and insisted they "show up with some class" for the FSU Women's Volleyball blood donation as a team.

Carrie had just gotten back to the apartment after witnessing the collapse of the north tower and was taken aback when Amber asked, "What's this about showing up with some class?"

"It's about RESPECT," Carrie had snapped. "Don't you think we can show some respect today for all the people who have died…and might in the near future?"

"Okay, okay," said Amber.

She had never seen Carrie as upset and angry as when she came back from the Union.

"Those guys might be in harm's way before this is over," cried Carrie as she looked at the continual reruns of each unbelievable event of the day.

"Who?" asked Amber.

"Jeff and Dave!" she shouted. "Don't you see? They called up the Guard and sent them to Desert Storm last time. Wake up and smell the coffee, Amber. This changes everything going forward. This is our Pearl Harbor!"

Amber went over and sat down by Carrie. She was usually the one to collapse and cry over a loss or bad day. Carrie was the rock. Today, she held Carrie's hand and pulled her over to cry on her shoulder.

◆◆◆

Carrie looked around the front lawn of the Blood Center. At 3:15, people were still arriving to give blood from a request on the Eyewitness noon news.

And there, near the end of the line, were Jeff and Dave. Dave saw her, nudged Jeff, and they both waved. Carrie motioned for them to join the team. Dave and Jeff were talking, then almost arguing. Finally, Jeff looked at Carrie. Dave gave him a shove. Dave pointed to his place in line and grinned.

Jeff ambled past the team. Normally, he'd be teased for coming to talk to Carrie after "The Hatchet Incident," as it had come to be affectionately known on the team. A few of the freshmen players seemed to have a crush as he walked by. Jeff seemed embarrassed to be making the walk over, obviously on Dave's urging. Carrie couldn't resist.

"Mr. Hanford, would you like to join our team today?" Carrie teased as he approached her.

"No, Hatchet, I think I've given enough blood on behalf of the team already," Jeff said. "I'm here for a bigger cause today. Just thought I'd come over to tell you and the team we think it's a classy thing you're doing. People in the community know it's a FSU group out here today. You did us proud." With that,

Jeff gave the others in the team a wave and ambled back to Dave.

"Garrett Hamilton will have him running for office if he keeps that up," said Amber.

"I love Garrett, but Jeff's too good for politics," said Carrie before she could catch herself.

Amber looked at her with a shake of the head but seemed to know better than to tease her today.

◆◆◆

The 5:00 p.m. Eyewitness News was wall to wall with the 9/11 story, but finished with a short segment from the local blood bank. The reporter had noted all the crowd and then focused on the FSU women's volleyball team showing up in strength. Their co-captain, Carrie Station, was in a short interview, saying, "It was just one small thing we could do on such a tragic day."

As the news ended at 5:30, they showed a clip of Jeff talking to Carrie as the camera panned the long line of the day.

At 5:32, Jeff got a call from Amy. "Well, looks like you and Carrie got FSU well represented today," Amy snapped.

"I was just up there for a minute, then went back to the end of the line with Dave," said Jeff.

Aren't you worried about some front lines I might be in soon?

"Amy, what are you doing tonight at 7:00?" he asked, hoping to disarm her. "There's a memorial candle lighting event at Prexie's Pond tonight at 7:00. Would you like to go?"

"Why? Aren't you already going with the volleyball team?" Amy shot back.

"I don't know who's going," Jeff snapped. "AMY, do you want to go?"

"No, I've had enough wallowing in tragedy. I'm going to call Mom and go home this weekend since they've cancelled the football game for Saturday."

"Fine," said Jeff. "Talk to you later."

◆ ◆ ◆

The mild wind of the morning had died down. Amber walked with Carrie under the Campanile as the late afternoon sun hit the new facing on the top of its foundation bricks. They had waited all summer for the specially matched bricks. They were going to have a ceremony on Homecoming week at the end of September to place a time capsule inside the last few bricks of the new facing.

"Well, they'll be able to put a new note in the history of 2001 when they put the time capsule in," said Amber.

"I think September 11, 2001 is going to be a defining day like December 7, 1941 was for my grandparents' generation," said Carrie, as she looked ahead at the crowd gathering over at Prexie's Pond.

As they approached, they could see the boxes of candles being handed out at each corner by student senators.

Amber nudged Carrie. "It's Jeff and Dave," she said.

Carrie looked up and said nothing as they continued walking toward the long east side of the rectangular pond.

Dave and Jeff were walking toward the shorter north side of the pond. Like many students, they were wearing small American flag lapel pins that had disappeared from shelves at the campus drug store and Walmart by late afternoon.

"I've got to say hi to Dave," said Amber as they arrived at their side.

"Dave? I thought you weren't ever talking to him again after that freshman year date?"

"He seems to have grown into a decent guy since he joined the Guard. And Jeff's been a good influence on him, too. Just stay here, okay?" Amber said before Carrie could stop her.

Amber walked over to Dave while Jeff took a couple of steps back to look at his cell phone, leaving them privacy space. Then Amber turned to Jeff, and talked to him a few seconds. Jeff looked up at Carrie and slowly walked around the pond.

"What's that about, Rockhead?" asked Carrie when he arrived. "I thought she hated him."

"She said to tell you it's 'Support the Troops Night.'"

"Okay," said Carrie. "We'll share a candle."

God, help me get through this.

The service started as dusk set in at 7:30. There was a muted floodlight under the small, portable lectern on the south side. The service began with Dean Winters addressing the students, faculty, and some community that had come. It was now two to three deep all the way around the pond.

"Today, terrorists attacked America. As President Bush said, we've seen the face of evil. It was shocking, brutal, and unprovoked. It killed people from *over 50 nations* that lived and worked in those buildings or died on those planes. This was not just an attack on us. They indiscriminately killed people from those nations, too. I know many of our international students are also here tonight to mourn losses.

"The people who did this today seem to be afraid of our freedoms. Freedom of speech, thought, religion, and opportunity. Where there has been a misplaced hatred today, we must try to understand and work to curb this chasm in our international community. At the same time, we also must be firm and resolute for our country's safety and future.

"Tonight, we're gathered here for a memorial service to be followed by a candle lighting ceremony around the pond. The service is multi-denominational. Before we begin that service, I'd like to have you join me in a song that was sung by Congress today on the steps of The Capitol, *God Bless America.* We'll be led by one of the great music majors of FSU and a good friend for 25 years, Mavis Hendricks."

The President then stepped aside and Mavis stepped forward. Jeff and Carrie looked at each other in surprise. They'd never heard her sing. Mavis then opened acapella with an operatic voice that sent chills down Carrie's spine. Everyone joined in singing. None present would forget the impact and distinct meaning of the song for each of them that night.

A Catholic priest and Lutheran pastor from the campus ministry led the memorial service with short comments and passages from the Bible.

The priest commented on the trials in life that Jesus warned about. He then read John 16:33: "I have told you all this so that you may have peace in me. Here on earth you will have many trials and sorrows. But take heart, because I have overcome the world."

The pastor commented on trials and tragedies suffered for thousands of years. She then read Psalm 25:2-3: "In you I trust, O my God. Do not let me be put to shame, nor let my enemies triumph over me. No one whose hope is in you will ever be put to shame, but they will be put to shame who are treacherous without excuse."

They were followed by a local rabbi who said he'd be reading the 23rd Psalm. He invited them to join in, if they desired. After he started, voices from all sides of the pond joined in. Several students close to the podium held hands. Others noticed and soon all were joining hands around the pond. Jeff reached out to Carrie. For the first time since the tornado, they held each other's hand.

The Lord is my shepherd; I shall not want. He maketh me to lie down in green pastures: he leadeth me beside the still waters. He restoreth my soul: he leadeth me in the paths of righteousness for his name's sake. Yea, though I walk through the valley of the shadow of death, I will fear no evil: for thou art with me; thy rod and thy staff they comfort me. Thou preparest a table before me in the presence of mine enemies: thou anointest my head with oil; my cup runneth over. Surely goodness and mercy shall follow me all the days of my life: and I will dwell in the house of the Lord forever.

Around the pond, many students kept holding hands, some let go. Carrie started to let go but Jeff, with his eyes still on the pond in front of them, pulled back slightly to keep holding hands. He gently squeezed her hand.

Quietly, volunteers and student senators walked down the lines on all sides of the pond, lighting candles. Jeff took their candle off the grass. He and Carrie held it together. It was dark now. As each candle was lit, reflections of their light could be seen on the water around the pond.

Dean Winters stepped back to the podium with the three religious leaders to his right. First Winters, then each of the others, stepped forward with their final comments.

The president said, "Let these candles be a memorial to all who died today. May we never forget those who died suddenly, those who died in service to others, and those who may have died trying to stop these acts. " He held up his candle and all followed.

The rabbi said, "Let these candles be a tribute from us going forward to maintain our freedoms of religion, thought, and gathering peacefully in the name of mankind." He held up his candle and all followed.

The priest followed with, "Let these candles be a tribute to maintaining our freedoms of speech, press, life, liberty, and an unselfish pursuit of happiness. He held up his candle and all followed.

The pastor said, "Let these candles be a signal to the world that our faith, freedoms, and traditions will continue." She held up her candle, all followed and she said, "Now may we hold our candles silently for a minute of silence."

In the darkness, with heads bowed, Jeff gently gripped Carrie's hand tighter.

"Thank you. This concludes the memorial," said the pastor. "Please extinguish your candles but let their light shine in your hearts forever." She held her hand up behind her candle, blew it out, and put it down in the grass in front of her.

As others began to blow out their candles, Jeff and Carrie blew theirs out together. Jeff let go of her hand. Carrie looked over for Amber, who still had their candle lit. She looked across at Carrie, gestured with her thumb at Dave and the car beyond. She blew out their candle and waved good night to Carrie.

"Guess I'm walking home alone," Carrie said. "Looks like today has brought together more people than you'd expect." She smiled and motioned toward Dave and Amber walking to his car, holding hands.

"Yeah, guess I'm hoofing it too," chuckled Jeff. "Mind if I walk with you?"

My God, yes. Tonight I'd...

"Sure," said Carrie. "Can we just sit here for a while first?"

While most were leaving, some stayed to talk and hug. Several were crying and holding each other.

It was a remarkable yet not surprising scene for all they'd experienced that day and the memorial's moving ending.

"Thanks," Carrie said as they sat down. "Do you know yet whether you're on alert or anything?"

"No alert for us," said Jeff. "Most of the Air Guard was called in or put on standby today. They don't expect any commercial or private planes flying for several days. Dave and I just have to keep our cell phones on or by us 24/7 for a few days."

Jeff reached over and put his hand on top of hers where she was leaning back on the grass.

They sat silently for several minutes. They were now alone by the pond except for volunteers excusing themselves as they came by putting candles back in boxes. Soon they were gone, leaving Carrie and Jeff all alone.

"We'd better get going," Carrie said in a quiet whisper. "You've got others waiting for you."

I'd stay here all night if you asked me.

Jeff made no move to get up. He sat there, holding her hand.

"Jeff?" Carrie whispered.

"Okay," Jeff solemnly said as he got up.

A crescent moon was low in the evening sky as they walked up the mild slope to the Campanile and past it.

"They had a hit out on us but we didn't think it was here at home," Jeff said as he shook his head. "Seems like the tectonic plates of history are shifting under us today."

He looked at Carrie and laughed softly. "That was a real Rockhead observation. Aren't you going to give me a shot for that one?"

"Not tonight, Jeff," Carrie said as she looked back at him with tears in her eyes.

They stopped under the light at the crossroads between their apartments.

Jeff looked at Carrie, reached out, and they

hugged each other as so many others had that night. It felt natural. It felt right.

Then, as Jeff pulled back, he stopped and held Carrie. Slowly, he pulled her up to him and kissed her lips.

Carrie put her arms around his neck and kissed him back—a long, passionate kiss.

He gently pulled back to lean his forehead against hers. Their noses touched. They both closed their eyes as they held each other.

Finally, Jeff let go of their embrace.

"I'll see you Thursday in class," said Jeff.

"Okay," Carrie whispered.

Jeff turned and walked down the hill. Carrie watched him walk away, then walked east to her apartment.

21

Top Secret Clearance

WEDNESDAY, SEPTEMBER 12, 2001 was the beginning of "The New Normal" at FSU…and in America.

Carrie had arrived early for her *Advanced Systems Management* class. Computer/info systems majors had declined at FSU in the fall of 2000, after the "dot-com bust" of the stock market in the spring of 2000. It had been sobering for many who saw the IT major and field as booming the year before. Now, a year later, students were coming back to the major in modest numbers.

"Carrie, do you think this will affect jobs next spring, again?" asked Nancy as she sat down next to her.

We have empty skies, commercial flights cancelled for the near term, and Manhattan has a smoking pile that may have some survivors in it. Get a grip, sister.

"I don't know. Better ask the professors," answered Carrie.

Carrie went to two more of her computer/IT classes on Wednesday morning. She was still more upset about 9/11 and what it was doing to people right around her. She'd talked to her folks the night before. Westham Energy would have to be even more vigilant on physical security.

After class, she looked up at the Campanile as she walked to the Union.

Jeff kissed me last night like he loved me. Should I call him?

No, he said see you in class on Thursday, and just walked away. Like it was a handshake. You're a NEANDERTHAL, Rockhead!

◆ ◆ ◆

"Hey, Carrie, can I join you?" Dave asked.

It was the noon hour bustle in the café at the Union and Carrie had decided to have some comfort food, a burger, for lunch.

"Sure, have a seat. Amber didn't make it home last night," Carrie said with a sly look.

She called me this morning and told me where she'd been. With you, Beavis.

"Yeah," said Dave, blushing. "She came over to my apartment after the candle lighting. I guess she forgot to go home."

"So, you're not on her shit list anymore, huh?" teased Carrie.

"Guess not," Dave said as he smirked with a mouthful of hamburger.

Why do I put up with these smart asses?

"How about you?" said Dave with a mouthful of hamburger. "Seen Jeff? I heard him come in the apartment but when he, ah, figured our one bedroom was occupied, I heard him leave."

"Well, did you check with Amy?" Carrie snapped. She picked up her Coke, took her half done sandwich, dumped it in the trash can, and headed for the library.

❖❖❖

Jeff came in and slowly walked down his row. Carrie kept looking at the front Power Point as she pretended to take copious notes of the title slide.

"Hey, Carrie."

"Hi." She'd flipped her notebook back to check her notes from the previous Thursday since they'd missed on Tuesday, 9/11.

"You get Tuesday's notes from anyone yet?" asked Jeff, hesitantly.

"No, I was in the Union with the two guys who owe me notes yet from so many skipped Friday classes on Guard weekends," said Carrie, not looking up.

The professor walked in and proceeded to cover the 19th century evolution of imperialism in the Mideast in Cyprus and Egypt.

Carrie walked out quickly at the end of class. Jeff caught up to her on the sidewalk to the library.

"Carrie, I'm sorry," said Jeff. "I didn't mean to seem to take you for granted on class notes. I'm sorry."

Carrie stopped and replied in a furious, low voice, "Sorry about expecting class notes? You think I'm upset about taking me for granted about CLASS NOTES? Jeff Hanford, you ARE a sorry son of a bitch!"

Carrie pivoted and walked quickly toward the library.

For the final three months of the semester, Jeff never brought up the kiss. So, Carrie never brought it up either.

❖❖❖

THURSDAY AFTERNOON
SEPTEMBER 13, 2001

"Hello, Maureen," Carrie said as she saw the caller ID. "How are you?"

"I'm just sick with this, Carrie. It's so huge, so tragic," Maureen Hamilton said. "Garrett's even rattled, but he won't admit it. How are you? What's up for Jeff? Are they on alert?"

"No, they weren't on Tuesday night when we all ran into each other at the memorial at Prexie's Pond," said Carrie.

"Oh, I heard that was so moving. I called Mavis

on Wednesday and she said Dean Winters had asked her to sing at the opening of the program."

"Mavis was so good. Jeff and I never knew that about her," Carrie said. "That operatic voice for *God Bless America.* People started singing along with her, all around the pond. Then when the rabbi started to read the 23rd Psalm, most everyone started saying it along with him, all around the pond. Then, with the crowd three deep at least, Jeff and I had to share a candle. When all the candles were lit, the reflection on the pond was…"

"You were there with Jeff," said Maureen. "That had to be special."

"It was kind of spontaneous, really," Carrie forced a laugh. "Amber, my roommate, ditched me for Dave, Jeff's roommate and buddy from the National Guard. Jeff walked over to keep me company, I guess."

"How about your guy Brad?"

"He wasn't there, Carrie said. "We broke up the Saturday night after I saw you and Garrett for the Website Task Force meeting."

"Oh, Carrie, I'm so sorry, honey."

"It's all right. Really. We didn't see each other all summer. We agreed by phone on Memorial Day that we both wanted to date around for the summer. That was really the beginning of the end."

"I'm sorry, it's still so hard."

"Dating around was good," said Carrie. "I finally

got asked out by my high school crush, the star quarterback. Did you ever have a chance to go out with a guy who didn't give you the time of day in high school or college? And you finally did. And it wasn't a big deal? Like a confirmation that your life was better now."

"Oh, Carrie, you're too good," Maureen laughed. "I figured that out about my first love who dumped me after our senior year in high school. Thought I was going to die for a few weeks. Then the summer after my sophomore year at FSU, I saw him at a woodsy."

"Maureen Hamilton, at a woodsy!"

"Yes, I went to a woodsy. My halo's not that tight," Maureen said, serious again. "I got over him that night, too. So you're all right. How's Brad?"

"We're going to stay friends," said Carrie. "No bitterness or wondering where you stand going forward. We're good."

◆◆◆

"Carrie, it's Garrett. Do you have five minutes?" he said without waiting for an answer. "Maureen's on the other end listening in. I just got off the phone with Governor Wemberly. He's going to appoint me chair of a Governor's Terrorism Task Force. Probably be called the GTTF or STTF.

"I told him I'd be honored, but I had reservations. I told him the last year had taught me how much I didn't know about high tech, and websites. I told him

I'd take it on if he gave me latitude beyond the usual ones you'd expect. Head of National Guard, head of state's emergency management division, key industry CEOs, etc. I told him I wanted to appoint you to the task force and at least two to three key staffers like you who can explain the ramifications of the computer, internet, websites, and beyond. I told him I would not listen to one more report that's incomplete on its tech projections or be the chair for a bunch of CEO's who can't log on to the Internet!"

Wasn't that you a year ago, Garrett?

Carrie's throat was suddenly dry. "Governor, I'd be honored, but do you think I'm up for a state commission?"

"Carrie, damn it. They used our own planes, our freedom of movement, and our open culture against us!" barked Garrett.

"Garrett Hamilton, watch your tongue!" Maureen barked back.

"It's okay," said Carrie. "I know he's not mad at me.

"Garrett, they overstayed their damned visas and we didn't even call them or try to bring them in," said Carrie. "Jay Leno's right. If we issued them a Blockbuster's video rental card along with the visa's, they'd find them in a week for an overdue video!"

"You see, Maureen? I told you," said Garrett.

"Okay, Carrie, you're going to have to go through a top secret background check for access to the classified material. You know how sensitive some things are from your Westham internship. Some of this would chill your spine, but you're the type we need for this new commission. A sense of duty, integrity…and driven to make us safe again. I'm counting on you."

Garrett hung up before he really got Carrie's confirmation. Maureen called back later that afternoon and ironed things out for Garrett, once more. It was Sunday night, September 23rd. Carrie's background packet arrived the next day by Fed Ex. It was thick.

❖❖❖

"Jeff, you got a minute?" Carrie asked as they walked out of class. They hadn't exchanged much more than pleasantries for the last two weeks. She and Dave had quietly reconciled the next week in the Union when she apologized for her rudeness when asked about Jeff. He told her he thought she was exactly right, just overzealous. They laughed, hugged and were bantering the next day in class. But Jeff just listened and laughed, but didn't participate in it now.

He followed her out of class. She motioned toward the back hallway.

"I have something important. It's serious," she said. "I wouldn't ask it if I didn't need it."

Damn it, my hands are trembling. I don't want him to patronize me on this.

"What is it?" asked Jeff. "If you're in trouble, let's figure it out."

Damn it, Rockhead. I'm not pregnant!

"No, Jeff," she said, trying to hide her anger. "Garrett Hamilton has asked me to be on a top secret terrorism task force as a website and security specialist. I need references and you're in the National Guard. I don't have any government references except Garrett. So, will you be my other reference?"

"Yes, YES," he said. "That's the first good news I've heard on the home front in weeks."

"What do you mean?"

"We just had Guard last weekend. They don't know what to do except put more obstacles up for us to drive through on our way in the gates, and restrict family visits to the base. They'll make exceptions for special events like the Halloween party and Santa's visit at the Armory. That ought to stop al Qaeda."

Well, good, Rambo. Glad you've channeled all your emotions into one slot.

"Back to the background check," said Carrie as she looked behind them. "Here's the form. Please fill it out and mail it in as soon as possible to the FBI."

Jeff's eyes widened. "Carrie, you're going to be on a government terrorist task force."

"Yes. Send it to the FBI. Look, this is secret. Only you and my folks know I'm going through this check, okay? If I don't get approved, I don't serve on the task force."

"I'll fill it out tonight and drive it down to the post office," said Jeff.

"I'm glad they're doing something on the state level. Our General, the Commandant, has his secretary log him onto the Pentagon and FEMA secured connections. Our leaders are internet illiterates. And I'm glad Garrett's getting you. You're the type we need going forward. First Sgt. Fernandez is right. It's time to kick ass and take names."

"Okay. Thanks, Jeff."

"If you make the task force because of my lies and BS for your form, will you call me Rockhead again?"

He was giving her The Grin.

"YES, just fill it out, okay?"

I'd kick your nuts right now but it would ruin your future in the Guard.

◆◆◆

Carrie was announced as part of the Governor's Terrorism Task Force a week later. Maureen said the fast turnaround was a sign of how serious the times were now. Commandant (General) Keith Blairsford and John Hartman of Westham Energy were also on the task force. It was announced on local Eyewitness News and covered by every paper in the state, including Springfield's.

When Carrie came into class the next day, Jeff and Dave were in the back of the room doing their mock *Wayne's World* "we're not worthy" bows.

"Sit down and behave, you two, or I'll have the Governor put you on the no fly list," Carrie laughed.

Later, as she walked out of class ahead of Jeff, he caught up beside her.

"Glad the reference helped you get on the task force," Jeff said.

"Jeff, thanks for the background reference for the FBI. I really appreciate it. Now, I've got to get going," Carrie said

Jeff looked surprised that she didn't want to stay and talk to him.

She looked down and walked away from him at a brisk pace.

Rockhead, sometimes you're such a dumbass.

◆ ◆ ◆

The rest of the fall was like a blur for Carrie. The volleyball team had opted to have patriotic pre-game music instead of rock for warmups. When the curtain split now before the game, a four-person FSU ROTC/Guard group came out with a color guard.

Dave had lined it up at Carrie's request. He was the coordinator of the rotation and said it increased morale, competition for color guard, and dating life with volleyball players for the unit. Carrie and Dave were tight again.

The GTTF had its first meeting on Thursday, October 11, one month after 9/11, at the Capitol. The meeting was surprising for Carrie. She was one of the 12 "at the table" for the task force. They had a support staff of six. Two were like her, with IT/computer/website backgrounds. Maureen had called her to let her know she was the youngest member and first college student appointed to a state task force who'd gotten a top-secret security clearance.

She was assigned website and airport security gate support at the state level. The airports all had local commissions and Garrett wanted to have a better liaison with the mix of private security gate companies and airline gate contractors. To study that, he got Carrie on the expense account and had her fly to two airports each Friday or Saturday before the next meeting three weeks later on November 1st.

Her findings, with a first draft to Garrett, became part of the written report with virtually no changes.

She noted that the different airlines' security contractors were not consistent enough to avoid gaps in the future. She, along with others, recommended federalizing it under one organization. Garrett forwarded it to the NTTF, National Terrorism Task Force, after their November 1st meeting.

◆◆◆

"Carrie, this is Garrett. Look, I know this is short notice, but in two weeks a few of us are invited to the NTTF's national summit on Friday, Nov 30 through Sunday, December 2nd in D.C. They requested you be one of our quota from your website and airport gate reports. Did you get that? I didn't pull strings. You're going on your own merits. Maureen and I couldn't be more proud if it was one of our own kids. Can you go?"

◆◆◆

NOVEMBER 30, 2001

Carrie arrived at the airport early. She wanted to observe check-in, people, luggage, and ticket counters. And she didn't want to embarrass Garrett.

"Carrie, I'm glad you're on our team for this trip to the national summit," said John Hartman, CEO of Westham. "Your mom and dad are rightfully proud. I'll need to sit alone on the flight and catch up on the review materials. I'll see you at the sessions tonight."

Garrett had arrived late and asked Carrie to walk alone with him after checking in at the front.

"Watch security gate procedures today with our group, okay?" Garrett said quietly. "Drop back here and also at O'Hare. Stay three to four people behind our group to watch all of us go through. I've already told the others to disregard you as part of the process. You'll be seated next to me on our way to O'Hare."

◆◆◆

"Well, what did you see?" said Garrett after takeoff. He seemed to sense Carrie's nervousness. "You're not just here because I appointed you. They read your report on website security. You were the only one who said in plain English that we need to make our passwords more complex rather than 'hardening our security protocols.'"

Relieved, Carrie relaxed a little. "One, Commandant Blairsford got through security despite forgetting he had his jack knife in his pocket. He was cleaning his fingernails later in our seats. The gates are probably set too light for metal detection. We may need to recommend secret testing of systems—no heads up.

"Second, the gate people and their team lead recognized you and the general in his uniform. He was watching you more than his gate agents. One of them was looking sideways joking with the one who was taking our things off belts from the scanners. I don't think he was even looking down when my laptop went through. It could have been a gun.

"Three, when the lead agent came over to a passenger complaining about going through a gate, he accidently stepped on the multi-plug power bar and it turned off the gate! It probably took a minute before they realized it was the power bar. He was griping to one of his gate agents that the damned machine was probably on the fritz again."

Garrett chuckled. "Maureen's right. She told me you'd be smarter than some of us old dogs on this new hunt. Keep making notes and suggestions like that on any of this, okay?"

◆◆◆

ALEXANDRIA, VIRGINIA

That evening, Carrie joined a group from the

reception that had jokingly labeled themselves the *computer/web nerd team* as they attended the first program. It was a panel of experts for *Public and Private Sector Website Security*. The standout panelist was Lynn Franheiser, the FBI web security specialist. She was specific and more knowledgeable than any of the other panelists. Carrie talked to her afterward and asked for her card in case she needed to follow up. It would prove to be valuable later.

The next afternoon, she made sure she went to one of the breakouts.

Murdock, from the Chicago field office of the FBI. Your card listed you as a cyber specialist last summer.

Now, you're Agent Frank Murdock, a cyber-terrorism specialist. How convenient!

Murdock was on a panel on *Guarding National Infrastructure from Terrorism*. Carrie looked in from the hallway to avoid being seen. He was taking a seat at the panelists' table up front on the riser.

Suddenly, a very tall Army officer came walking toward the door. Carrie followed him in with her head down. Luckily, with sparse seating in the row behind him, she could pull a chair sideways so she could hide behind the tall brass. Murdock couldn't see her, but she could see the other three panelists. She kept her head down, writing through most of the panel.

His slide show was good. It showed al Qaeda efforts including the Y2K terrorist attempt at the

Canadian border in late December 1999. Then his slide came up with "other state-sponsored and non-state terrorists. Iran, Syria, and then, near his conclusion, there it was.

"This is a new one I've been following," Murdock said. "There is evidence that Russian hackers, who may be state-sponsored, independent, or from the Russian mob, are now a threat to the US. Remember, Putin was the first world leader to unilaterally call Bush and offer to help in the war on terror. Putin told Bush that they know what it is like to deal with terrorists."

The next slide came up. There it was. Virtually word for word, it was Carrie's in-house write-up for Hartman at Westhaven to forward to the FBI after their meeting with Frank Murdock the previous summer in Springfield.

Murdock was using a brief version of what Carrie had given him on the *Def Con* hackers convention meeting last summer. But he cited himself as the source.

If I could shoot a laser through the General in front of me, you'd be toast, Murdock.

The panel was over. The moderator asked for questions. There were several for the other panelists but Murdock hadn't had any…yet.

"Time for one more question."

Carrie raised her hand and was recognized by the moderator. She stood up.

"Agent Murdock, what do you think about concerns that the Russian mob, having extorted ransom money from Putin already, might be a threat to sell hacked information to al Qaeda in the future?" asked Carrie in a steady, loud voice. Heads turned throughout the ballroom.

Murdock's face turned pale. He slowly turned the shared microphone on the table toward him.

"We're unaware of any attempts," he replied hesitantly, "but we're pursuing avenues through our liaison with Russian intelligence."

The breakout was over. Carrie had moved her chair so she could see him. Murdock stared at Carrie. She stared back with angry eyes, then slowly smiled. Murdock got up, said his quick thanks to the others, and then walked toward the side aisle as if he had another urgent session to attend.

Before Carrie could get up, the Army officer ahead of her had turned around.

"How did you find out about the Russian mob extorting Putin?" asked the one-star general.

Well, here it goes. I may be in an orange jumpsuit soon.

"Public conversations at the Def Con hackers conference last summer, sir," Carrie said. "My website instructor attends it each year and told me about it afterwards. She said it sounded like the extortion payments started under Yeltsin and were continuing under Putin."

I'm not telling you about Westham Energy. I'll CYA for Hartman before I spill that.

"What's your name?" asked the general.

"Carrie. Carrie Station, sir," Carrie said, trying to hide her nerves.

"Do you have a card?"

"Yes, sir." Carrie dug out the GTTF business card with her name and the title, *Website Specialist and Airport Security Liaison.*

"Carrie, who are you working for now?" he asked as he handed her his card.

"I'm a senior at Freeman State University, sir. Majoring in computer and information science with a minor in history."

"You're good. Garrett Hamilton has a good reputation and integrity," he said with a steady gaze. "I hope you're applying for work with our national intelligence community. It's going to have a lot of growth and we can't find enough good, young computer experts for this war on terror. Recruits who can understand and talk geo-politics will be really valuable. And you caught Murdock at his game," he said with a chuckle.

"Thank you, sir. That's flattering and an honor to hear that from you," she said as she looked at the general's title: *US Army Intelligence & National Intelligence Agencies Liaison.* "Garrett Hamilton told me to apply for those positions. I'll certainly consider it, sir.

"If I could, sir, I think the FBI's Lynn Franheiser, who spoke on last night's panel, is a good young expert to seek out for your liaison work. I think she'd be valuable as you begin to integrate all these data and communication platforms that can't or won't trade information now. I think the new Director, Mueller, is a great improvement. He at least has a computer on his desk."

The general laughed.

"I agree, I agree," he said, as he turned serious. "Listen, Carrie, if you're in this room, you had to pass the basic top secret background check. We're revamping the testing and lie detector protocols for future national intelligence job applicants. We used to wash out any applicant who admitted to hacking before or who lied about hacking.

"You remind me of my daughter", he said with a smile. "The weekend after 9/11, she drove home. At breakfast, she told me the US intelligence establishment had to wake up. Hackers are everywhere in college dorms. It was no longer an occasional kid with the eccentric knack. It's like an underground hobby club now. We'd better hire some of them instead of the less competent ones. We're at war."

"She's pretty accurate, sir," Carrie said carefully.

"Wait and take the national security test after February 1st. By then we're going to have a policy revision for the lie detector tests. We'll start hiring some hackers...IF they are honest about it and if it wasn't something too criminal. Hell, we've been hiring the plea bargain hackers for years."

"Sir, I know someone who hacked the FSU website before Y2K, but only to download and save her grades in case the system had a Y2K crash," Carrie said as she looked down at her notebook. "Later, the Dean of FSU asked her...gave her permission to hack the university's Foundation website so he could be sure it was safe for online donations."

The general looked over his glasses and winked at her. "Tell your friend to tell the truth about those two incidents, and in just the way you described it, for her benefit." He rose and shook hands with her.

"Yes, sir, I will. Thank you so much."

Thank you, God. I won't be playing volleyball in prison after all.

◆ ◆ ◆

It was a heady and sometimes intimidating weekend for a senior in college. Carrie wrote her summary along with several that Garrett suggested. To her astonishment, he had them submit it as co-authors.

Those recommendations after the summit were reviewed and adopted by all in the state's terrorism task force. Garrett also forwarded it to a general in US Army intelligence who had requested it after the summit. Several of Carrie's recommendations were not only amongst the consensus for *The 9/11 Commission Report,* parts of it were word for word from her recommendations.

22

Finality

DECEMBER 14, 2001

FINAL TIME

CARRIE WALKED ACROSS College Street to Chip's Brew House for a large coffee to go. As she walked back out, the Christmas lights were still glowing with a half-hour to sunrise. It had become her ritual for finals this year. Coffee, one last study of notes, and then to the final.

As she walked up the college hill past the trees in business windows, she turned on her portable CD player in her parka pocket. It was a Christmas CD her mom had gotten her several years before. It had Sinatra through NSYNC doing Christmas classics. She turned the corner with the boy band harmonizing *Merry Christmas, Happy Holidays.*

As she started up the diagonal sidewalk on campus, she could see several of the dorm windows with Christmas trees. She smiled and thought of her grandparents as Sinatra came on with *Have Yourself a Merry Little Christmas.* It was Friday, her last final before her last Christmas break. Graduation was next spring.

Sipping her coffee as she walked past the snow-covered pine trees on her way to the library, she was hit by a surprising feeling from the song. Nostalgia. Not just for old times. For two years ago, one year ago. Before 9/11.

An hour later, she walked out and headed toward Fleener Hall. The campus was covered with two inches of snow from earlier in the week. She had her parka hood up. It was 24 degrees with a 10 mph wind in her face from the south. It added a bite as she walked over for her last final before break.

This will be the last final I'll have with Jeff. He's graduating and going to law school. With Amy.

The finality of times she'd be seeing Jeff had hit her last week while they talked before their last lecture for the class. She mentioned Bush's "war cabinet pictures" on *Vanity Fair's* December cover and the war in Afghanistan. Jeff told her Secretary of State Colin Powell was the only one he trusted in the group. She pretended to listen but felt a deep sadness.

Jeff had been consumed recently talking about the war—the quick fall of the Taliban government, our tactical mistakes, too few military troops vs. CIA operatives on the ground, Al Qaeda on the run, and finding bin Laden. This was a different Jeff than she'd known in October when he became quiet while Dave and she bantered. He was Army reserve but he'd never sounded like this. Well, he'd soon be in law school and he could stew about the war. If he didn't get called up like Desert Storm.

The usual mix of test anxiety and euphoria of finals week and going home for Christmas break was muffled this year for many during the Christmas season of 2001. Carrie was surprised that she was nostalgic, sad, and a little bit worried about the future.

She still couldn't believe how much had happened since 9/11. She was the youngest member appointed to the Terrorism Task Force, got a top-secret security clearance while still in college, and was sought after for her opinion on computer and website issues.

Garrett and Maureen Hamilton had both become mentors. She'd come a long way for a girl who thought she wasn't going to be much of a computer whiz when she was a freshman.

As Carrie walked into class, there were only a few seconds to say hi to Jeff in the back row seats, then the proctor handed out the exams promptly at 9:00. She smiled and silently mouthed the words, "Good luck" to him. He nodded back with a smile but a serious, almost sad look in his eyes.

Carrie walked up and handed in her final at 9:50. She'd rushed through her last page of questions quickly, hoping he'd be there, talking on his cell but waving at her to wait like he had earlier that fall.

In the hallway, she turned to look down by the staircase. She'd just watched Jeff walk out about three minutes earlier. He'd given her a hesitant look, as if he wanted to say something but with the strictness of finals, he just gave her an affectionate nod. He walked up to hand in his test and walked out with his head down, seeming forlorn instead of the usual relieved look after handing in a final. They'd exchanged that relieved look so many times for two years. And she realized the moment she'd been dreading the last two weeks had hit.

Today, Jeff wasn't there. He was gone.

That may have been the last time I'll see Jeff. Ever.

Carrie walked back to her apartment and began packing. Erin had left earlier. She had a quick sandwich with Amber before Amber left. Carrie was tired from studying and talking to Amber and Erin late the night before. As she waved at Amber from the upstairs window, she felt alone. She lay down for what she thought would be a short nap. She woke up near dusk, still feeling tired and funky.

"Girl, you need a shower," she said as she walked over to the CD/FM radio. She turned on one of Amber's favorite CD's…loud. A few minutes later she stepped into the shower. "One more trek to the Hofhaus later tonight!" she laughed as if she were denouncing one of her faults.

But as the warm water ran over her face and head, she heard the end of "Good Riddance" by Green Day.

The haunting song's lyrics and beautiful music hit her hard.

Carrie looked down with water washing over her hair and cried. She slid down the shower wall, sat under the water, and sobbed, "Jeff's gone. I never got to say goodbye."

She stopped sobbing, embarrassed that she'd had a meltdown and thankful she was alone. She sat with the water running over her for several more songs before she finished her shower and went into the bedroom. She looked in the mirror as she dried her hair.

"Okay, buck up cowgirl." she said, angry at her self-pity. "You were lucky to have a great guy as a good friend. Half of the team envied you because you had a boyfriend and also another guy, a good friend, you could talk to and tease. No one else in your world had that. And now, you have this career and future in front of you with the Task Force." *Be sad, then get over it. Get on with your life.*

Carrie did more packing for the rest of the evening. She would be taking the short flight home tomorrow instead of the usual four-hour ride back with her folks or on the bus. She was flying home at the governor's insistence, paid for by the task force. He wanted her to fly several more times, at task force expense, to meetings on national computer security as well as her Christmas and spring break trip home, not to a beach.

It was work for the task force, to monitor how well she thought people, equipment, and policies worked at airport gates. He'd also asked her to make one stop at the power company at home to talk with the head of the computer systems department, this time in her capacity as a member of the task force. She was to find out what they had done since 9/11 to tighten their security of physical and data systems as well as what they felt was needed in the future.

Carrie had asked her folks not to schedule anything for dinners or family events for the first few days home since there were 10 days until Christmas. It was a great long Christmas break this year.

On her first few days home, she wanted to work on the website and airport security problems the governor had told her to research. In her new surreal world, she was a senior in college with a top-secret clearance, receiving stipend and reimbursement checks as a member of the Governor's Task Force on Terrorism. It was both exciting and humbling how her life, career prospects, and America's future had changed since that day 14 months ago when she'd met Garrett & Maureen.

◆◆◆

ONE MORE TREK TO THE HOFHUAS

It was 11:00 p.m. Carrie had finished as much packing as she needed for home but didn't get time to shop. She'd have to do that when she got home.

"Hell with it. I'll throw some of the rest of this in and wash it at home. Time for a beer at the Hofhaus," she said as she turned off the TV. She'd gone there last year on the Friday night of Christmas break and it had been great. Many of the students had stayed there for another beer rather than drive or fly home right after finals.

It was 11:15 and a gentle snow fell as she walked into the Hofhaus. With the Christmas lights on in campus town and the snow, it was a beautiful sight. She was still a little wistful, nostalgic with this last Christmas break. *Well, a couple of brewskies should help that*, Carrie thought as she walked in.

The familiar loud crowd, music, and faux Bavarian tables with wood benches up front near the karaoke area were alive and merry as she walked in. And there, at a table off to the right, was Jeff, looking at her. He smiled, held up his beer stein, and motioned toward a seat across from him and Dave at the table for four. She was overjoyed that she'd see him but had to stifle her urge to run over and tell him how glad she was to see him…one more time.

A new pitcher of beer had just been put in front of Jeff. The waitress began to ask her what she wanted when Dave said drunkenly, "Give this young lady from the Governor's task force whatever she wants to drink!"

The guys laughed while Jeff looked at her sheepishly. After milking the moment while they quieted down, Carrie said in her best mimic of the woman across from Meg Ryan in the restaurant scene from *When Harry Met Sally,* "I'll have what he's having," as she pointed to his stein. The guys roared, and Jeff smiled that world-winning grin of his as the waitress plunked down a stein for Carrie amongst the boys.

"I'm glad I caught you, Jeff," Carrie said quickly after a short sip. "I want to wish you all the best in law school and wherever life takes you and Amy. I know Governor Hamilton's got plans for you when you get to his law firm in three years."

Dave got quiet and looked down. Jeff slowly looked up from his stein and said, "I'm not going to law school. I signed up to go active out of the Guard…to go to Afghanistan."

Carrie lowered her stein, stunned. The guys' eyes were on her.

Her thoughts swirled. She thought about his affectionate nod today, then the near sad look as he walked out.

"What's Amy think about all this?" Carrie blurted out before she could catch herself.

"Amy told me it was stupid. I can't do this—it

would ruin *her* plans." said Jeff. "We had a big argument after Thanksgiving break when I told her I'd decided to put off law school; it was time to serve my country. When I said that's what I'd decided, she said, 'Well, do it without me. I didn't sign up for this.' We broke up that Monday night."

Carrie remembered Jeff being different and looking serious these last few weeks—unshaven and looking tired when he walked into classes. She thought it was the pressure of his final semester, law school coming up, or maybe Amy being snarky about something. It was different but she didn't ask about it.

They'd both been careful with each other after the night they walked back from the 9/11 memorial service at Prexie's Pond. After he'd kissed her. It had changed things.

"Jeff, don't do this!" Carrie said. "You could stay in the reserves. Wait and see if they call you up like they did for the Gulf War. Rockhead, you don't need to do this!"

Dave nodded his bowed head in agreement with her.

Jeff looked at her and shook his head. "These are extraordinary times. You were right about FDR's 3rd term in 1940. Extraordinary times call for changes and breaks from your plans, from traditions. And sacrifice," said Jeff. "You know how we talked on 9/11. This is *our* Pearl Harbor!

"What we do now and going forward matters for the future. This isn't just a war between countries anymore. This war on terrorism isn't going to end in just Afghanistan. Al Qaeda has followers there and elsewhere. We'll have to deal with this as a generational fight."

He leaned forward, elbows on the table, as he pointed to Carrie. "You said it in class before they said it at a Pentagon press conference. *We won't get to end this with a surrender ceremony on the USS Missouri.* It's too important and I'm not going to sit by and wait to be called up."

Several surrounding tables were watching and listening to Jeff's surprisingly impassioned speech. No one was singing karaoke. The TV above the bar was on mute with the cable news reports from the Battle of Tora Bora and hunt for bin Laden in the caves.

The song "Hero" by Julio Iglesias came on the overhead music.

Carrie glanced at the bar TV, then looked directly in Jeff's eyes and asked, "How soon is this happening?"

"I'm going active at the end of January or early February," he said. "They're ramping up quickly but want to have some of us new college grad reserves go active to Officer's Candidate School when it comes around. I called Garrett this afternoon. He didn't try to talk me out of it. He said there'd be a slot for me at his law firm after I get out and get through law school."

Jeff leaned forward and put his hand on Carrie's free hand resting on the table. "I'm so glad you're on the Governor's task force. What you're doing is important for this war on terror. We'll have to figure out how to be safer, more secure. You're part of this, too. I'm so glad we got to meet each other, to give each other a hard time, to become good friends."

Jeff stood up and pulled his coat on. "I've got to get up early, get packed, and leave tomorrow." Then he pulled Carrie up by the hand and gave her a hug. She was shocked and lost in the surprise of the moment.

Jeff held her gently by the shoulders as he said, "You've got my email. Let me know what you can from the task force and where you go after graduation. Garrett says you're going to be part of Homeland Security going forward, either here at the state or federal level, if he has anything to say about it."

Carrie was stunned, numb from the suddenness of all that he'd said.

She watched him say a quick goodbye to several other people and got a bear hug from Dave at the end of the table. Then he circled away from Carrie toward the entryway.

Suddenly, Carrie turned, grabbed her parka, and twirled it on over her shoulders. "Jeff, you can't go yet," she called out. Only the noise of clinking glasses and plates in the back of the Hofhaus could be heard.

Jeff turned around. He looked surprised to hear Carrie so loud and abrupt in a crowd. She walked around the end of the table to the doorway where he stood.

"Jeff, you can't just leave this way! *I LOVE YOU.* I don't want you to leave and never know that." She grabbed him by his lapels, pulled him toward her, and kissed him. Jeff kissed her back, a deep passionate kiss as he put his arms under hers and lifted her into him.

The front of the Hofhaus erupted into a roar of approval and clapping. Dave yelled, "It's about time!" Several others at the table whooped, "Yeah!"

Carrie and Jeff broke the embrace and suddenly realized what had happened. Carrie looked at Jeff with tears in her eyes and said, "I love you, Rockhead. You always make me so damned mad when I argue with you, but God help me, I love you."

"I love you too, Carrie. I've known it since the 9/11 memorial night." He looked above the bar at the big clock on the wall. It was 11:50 p.m.

Jeff grabbed Carrie's hand, turned, and gently pulled her toward the door to the sound of more yells and catcalls. "Carrie, we've got to be somewhere in 10 minutes."

We'd better be at one of our apartments in 10 minutes, Carrie thought.

But they weren't going there. Jeff held her hand and led her across the street to the campus. Soft, quarter-sized snowflakes gently fell with nearly three inches of snow on the ground now. As they walked up the gentle slope toward the center of campus, it was a winter wonderland. Jeff put his arm around Carrie's shoulder. She leaned into his side as they walked.

"I'm sorry if I embarrassed you back there," she said.

"Are you kidding? I nearly blurted out that I wanted to talk to you after finals today but I thought it would be a mistake," Jeff said as he looked at her. "I was afraid I might lose you as a friend. And who wants to love some Rockhead she's never even dated and he's going off to war?"

Carrie stopped, turned to Jeff, and grabbed him by the lapels again. "WHO? WHO? Me, Jeff, me! I love you and I want you to come back to me. Okay? Now where the hell are you taking me besides my place?"

Jeff laughed and held her again for a long kiss under a light near the library.

"There!" said Jeff. He pointed toward the Campanile. They had about 100 feet left to walk to get there, and it was just about to turn midnight.

Suddenly, Carrie got it. Her heart rushed as she broke into a trot with Jeff on the sidewalk.

As they arrived at the bottom of the Campanile,

Jeff turned and put his arms around Carrie. "I've got to kiss the woman I love, the love of my life, for all 12 chimes to make it official." Jeff pulled her into his arms as tears ran down her face.

She thought she'd never get to see him again.

The future was scary and unsure. But Carrie and Jeff kissed under a giant Christmas wreath on the side of the Campanile until all 12 beautiful chimes had ended.

ABOUT THE AUTHOR

The draft is the only lottery David Furneaux's ever won. But it gave him an assignment in Army intelligence with an infantry unit eight miles above Pearl Harbor. It gave him a deep appreciation for timely and shared intelligence between government units and the military.

David has interviewed thousands of people as a national recruiter and later as an oral historian for veterans' history projects. He realized during the journey, he loved helping people tell their stories.

He's a recovering history major, volunteers at a local veterans medical center, and is an independent. In recent years he has been a speaker on the Pearl Harbor attack, WWII, the Korean War, and Veterans Day commemorations at Honor Flight programs, libraries, veterans organizations, and community centers.

He feels 9/11 was the domestic Pearl Harbor for America's 21st century.

David lives in Iowa. He's married and is a proud parent and grandparent.

E-mail David at: info@DavidFurneaux.com

www.davidfurneaux.com

NUMBLAND SECURITY
THE SERIES

WATCH FOR

Book Two in the
Numbland Security™ Series
Coming in Fall 2018

BEFORE THE FIRE

Follow Carrie Station as she emerges as a college student with a top-secret clearance in the growing national security fight against terrorism after 9/11.

When she discovers Jeff Hanford has chosen going to the war on terror instead of law school, she finally tells him she loves him. And finds he loves her.

Jeff and Carrie decide not to go home for Christmas after finals. Instead, they choose to be together, to go on their first date, have their first dance, and find out there are a few…maybe a lot of things they don't really know about each other.

Will they want to take this surprise new love home to their shocked families? Will Carrie wait for Jeff as he goes off to OCS and Carrie goes back to finish college?

Then flash-forward to 10 years later as Carrie

becomes a star in national security while Jeff is swept away on deployments in never-ending wars since 9/11.

These are the dedicated people who've served us for over 15 years.

We need to know more about them.

◆◆◆

EXCERPT FROM CHAPTER ONE:

FIRST SNOW

CARRIE AND JEFF walked arm in arm in a winter wonderland. They'd known each other for two years, traded sarcastic remarks in front of Dave and others who saw the chemistry they'd denied.

"It's our first snow," Jeff said as the snow covered their boot prints from the Campanile.

"Rockhead, are you turning into a romantic on me?" Carrie laughed, then poked his side. In the past, when he'd gotten the better of her, she'd slugged him on the shoulder.

Carrie stopped and picked up some snow. As she packed it, Jeff ran ahead a few feet and grabbed his own handful of snow. Suddenly, he got hit with a snowball on the side of the head. Hard.

Carrie laughed when she hit him with a second one as she ran by.

"I'm going to kill you," he yelled as he threw his first snowball. It barely grazed her shoulder.

They continued their snowball fight as they ran down the sidewalk. At the crossroads, where they'd kissed just months before, Carrie stopped behind the streetlight and quickly packed another snowball.

"Here's for kissing me, then NOT saying anything about it, Rockhead!" Carrie yelled as she let loose with a fast one that barely missed Jeff's head.

He hit her boot as she tried to run away. She slipped on the wet edge of the sidewalk and fell into the snow, laughing.

"Gotcha," laughed Jeff as he squatted over her and rubbed snow in her face.

Carrie squealed and flipped him sideways onto the snow beside her. She pounced on top of his stomach and pinned his arms.

"Now, do you want to kiss me again? Huh? Huh?" she teased.

"Yeah. Yeah," Jeff wheezed with his chest heaving. "Forever."

"Good. That's settled," said Carrie as she leaned down and kissed his wet face. She took off her glove, gently wiped his face, then leaned forward and kissed him again.

Made in the USA
Columbia, SC
14 May 2018